HEAD SPINNERS

SIX STORIES TO TWIST YOUR BRAIN

THALIA KALKIPSAKIS

ALLEN&UNWIN

First published in 2011

Allen & Unwin
83 Alexander Street
Crows Nest NSW 2065
Australia
Phone: (61 2) 8425 0100
Fax: (61 2) 9906 2218
Email: info@allenandunwin.com
Web: www.allenandunwin.com

A Cataloguing-in-Publication entry is available from the National Library of Australia www.trove.nla.gov.au

ISBN 978 1 74237 345 4

Cover and text design by Design by Committee
Set in 12.5/17 pt Stemple Garamond by Midland Typesetters, Australia
This book was printed in February 2011 at McPherson's Printing Group, 76 Nelson Street, Maryborough, VIC 3465, Australia

10 9 8 7 6 5 4 3 2 1

HEAD SPINNERS

CONTENTS

To Mum, for listening.
And to Dad, for making
science interesting.

TICK-TOCK TIME MACHINE

1

'HAPPY BIRTHDAY, SQUIRT!' said Uncle Owen.

'Oh ... thanks,' I said, trying to forcing a smile.

The package was wrapped in creased, white tissue paper and was about twenty times smaller than the surfboard I'd wanted. If I hadn't known Uncle Owen better, I would almost have thought it was a *book*.

'Go on, Sam, open it!' Uncle Owen sat at the kitchen table, rubbing his hands together.

'Do you want a quick coffee?' Mum asked him.

'Nah thanks, Sis.'

Curiosity overtook my disappointment; I ripped the paper away, and frowned. 'Oh . . . thanks,' I said again, not in disappointment this time but in confusion. In my hands was a metal box with a digital screen, a tangle of wires at the back and a series of switches sticking out from the side. It looked like a homemade bomb.

'I know you asked for a surfboard,' said Uncle Owen, bouncing in his seat. 'But this'll help you catch the good waves. Trust me.'

'Right.' It was going to be pretty hard to catch any wave at all without a surfboard.

'What *is* that?' asked Mum, peering over the cereal box. I could see her scanning the wires, assessing whether to chuck my present out the window before it went beep and blew us all up.

'It's a clock, see?' Uncle Owen pushed a button and the display lit up with a faint humming sound. 'It synchronises itself by satellite and get this . . .' He raised his eyebrows, leaning forward. 'Each morning it reads data from the weather station at The Point. If conditions are good to catch a few waves then an alarm will go off.'

Mum rolled her eyes. 'Oh my lordy,' she sighed.

'If the weather's no good then there's no alarm and you get a bit more shut-eye!'

I cracked up laughing. Uncle Owen sure was out there, in a fun kind of way. He was famous for sleeping in and never seemed to have a proper job, but he was pretty smart too. 'Did you make this yourself?'

'Yeah.' Uncle Owen grinned and turned to Mum. 'Not bad for a surfie bum, eh?' He picked up the clock. 'It can do other things, too, like birthday reminders. And you can set the alarm to wake you up at a different time each day of the week.'

He pushed another button and TUE lit up on the display. 'What time did you get up today, Squirt?'

'Seven-thirty.'

Uncle Owen set the display to 07.30 and hit SET. 'And what time do you have to get up tomorrow?'

I shrugged. 'Ah . . . seven-thirty, I guess.'

Mum leaned forward. 'You could get up early and do some homework.'

I just looked at her.

'Oh well, never mind.' Uncle Owen laughed and put the clock back in front of me. 'You get the idea.'

'Get a move on, Sam, not long until the bus comes,' sighed Mum.

'Have a good one on Saturday, Squirt!' Uncle Owen ruffled my hair. 'Sorry again that I can't make it.'

'Nah, that's okay. Thanks, Uncle Owen.' This time it was easier not to sound disappointed.

As it turned out, that visit from Uncle Owen was the highlight of my day. It all went downhill from there.

When I headed for the bus, I was feeling great. A birthday coming up seems to have that effect on me, especially my own. So I did an extra big leap up the bus steps – skipping the first one to land on the second.

At least, that was what I *meant* to do.

In reality, my foot slipped on the edge of the step and twisted beneath me as I landed half-in, half-out of the bus. Everyone in *and* out of the bus got to see it and have a good laugh.

'Hey, kid, you alright?' asked the bus driver. He was out of his chair and grabbing at my arms, trying to help me up. 'Never seen anyone fall *up* those steps before.'

It would have been humiliating if I hadn't been in so much pain. My ankle felt as if it had been through a spin cycle in a washing machine loaded with rocks. Already I could feel it swelling.

'I'd better call your parents,' said the bus driver. 'What's the number?'

This was just perfect.

Mum took me to the doctors then I was stuck at home for the rest of the day, staring at the calendar and grumbling about bad timing. My birthday was in four days! I wanted to be out there sucking up the excitement and revelling in all the attention. Instead I was at home with a sprained ankle.

A sprained ankle, and a crazy clock.

2

Beep, beep, beep. It was seven-thirty.

I yawned, rolled over, and was surprised to find that the beeping was coming from my old clock. Where was the new one? I yawned again. Maybe Mum had got spooked by all the wires and taken it out of my room during the night.

Waking up slowly, I did my usual morning stuff. I was filling up my water bottle when I heard a knock at the back door, followed by the click and creak of it opening. Only one person comes in the back door.

'Happy birthday, Squirt!' said Uncle Owen.

I just stared at him. He was holding out a package that looked exactly the same as the one from yesterday, wrapped in the same creased, white tissue paper.

'Oh . . . ah . . . thanks,' I said, and looked

over at Mum. She smiled as if nothing weird was happening.

'Go on, Sam, open it!' said Uncle Owen, sitting at the kitchen table and rubbing his hands together.

'Do you want a quick coffee?' Mum asked.

'Nah thanks, Sis.'

This was really weird. I pulled at the tissue paper, pausing at a crooked bit of sticky tape that I remembered tugging at the day before. But that was just *crazy*. It couldn't be the same. Could it?

I tore again and my mouth dropped open . . . it was the *exact same clock*.

'I know you asked for a surfboard,' said Uncle Owen. 'But this'll help you catch the good waves. Trust me.'

I searched his face for the hint of a smile, a twinkle in his eye, anything to give the game away.

'What *is* that?' asked Mum.

It was the most bizarre feeling. I knew exactly what Uncle Owen was about to say: *It's a clock, see.*

'It's a clock, see?' he said and pushed a button. 'But you don't have to worry about setting the time. This clock'll . . .'

As they kept chatting, I looked from Mum to Uncle Owen then back to Mum again. It couldn't be yesterday again, surely. That simply wasn't possible. Yesterday, Uncle Owen had given me the present and I'd gone to catch the bus . . .

I froze for a second then breathed in. *My sprained ankle wasn't hurting.*

Not. One. Bit.

It wasn't puffy or even slightly tender. The bandage was gone.

I took another breath, as Uncle Owen's familiar words drifted to me. 'What time did you get up today, Squirt?'

I swallowed then whispered, 'Seven-thirty.'

Uncle Owen changed the display to 07.30 and hit SET. 'And tomorrow?'

But I couldn't say it. Dumbly, I shook my head.

Mum leaned forward. 'You could get up early and do some homework.'

In a daze, I just looked at her.

'Oh well, never mind.' Uncle Owen put the clock in front of me. 'You get the idea.'

'Get a move on, Sam, not long until the bus comes,' sighed Mum.

It was the strangest feeling – watching the world happen around me and knowing what was going to happen next. Walking out to the bus there were a lot of things that I hadn't noticed the first time round, of course, but also lots that I had. *A car goes toot, then in the distance there is the sound of a siren.* Just like the day before, I saw an old lady almost pulled over by a puppy on a lead. The puppy chose the exact same spot to squat. I *knew* it was going to do that, but seeing it happen for real made my head spin.

One thing was different from yesterday, though.

Me.

I was completely freaked out. I could barely think straight, let alone remember my thoughts from the day before. And I must have been walking slightly faster because I caught a set of pedestrian lights, crossing straight away, when yesterday I'd had to wait. When the bus door opened, I frowned at the step and bit my lip. I lifted my leg carefully and stepped up without anything going wrong. The bus driver didn't even glance at me as I passed. Feeling weird in a whole new way, I walked down the aisle. I'd made it, escaped from my sprained ankle, broken through to the other side . . . It was a relief to suddenly *not* know what was going to happen next.

When my friend Rodney slipped into the seat next to me, I summoned up the courage to ask, 'What day is it?'

He laughed. 'Feels like Thursday at least, doesn't it?'

He'll say Wednesday, I thought. *It has to be Wednesday*.

'Sorry, Sam, it's only Tuesday,' sighed Rodney.

After that I just looked out the window – watching a world happen around me that had happened before. I'd made it onto the bus, at least, so I wasn't stuck at home. But this was another Tuesday alright.

Tuesday Take Two.

3

For the rest of the morning I was in a daze, staring at the people doing stuff around me but not really joining in. I was in shock, I guess. I couldn't stop thinking how close I'd come to *not* being there . . . to being at home with a sore ankle.

In some ways it felt more like a second chance than time travel. After all, it was only one day. Even though I'd managed to escape my accident on the bus, I failed a maths test because I was so spaced out. That evened things up, I figured.

But, as Tuesday went by, and the morning drifted further into memory, I started thinking that maybe I'd imagined it. It had just been a weird kind of extended déjà vu where I'd *thought* everything had happened before. It was a relief to go to bed that night with the promise of a fresh new day. Wednesday was waiting just on the other side of sleep. I rested my head on my pillow. Soon, everything would be okay.

Except, the next morning . . .

No, scrub that. The *next time I woke up* it was Tuesday all over again.

I didn't have to ask anyone what day it was. By then I knew the script by heart. It would almost have been boring if a churning sense of panic hadn't begun to grow inside me. To repeat a day once was strange, but I was living through Tuesday for *the third time*.

They say tomorrow never comes, but this was ridiculous. What if it kept happening forever? Would I start to look older while everyone else stayed the same age?

I still didn't know what was causing it, but I did have an idea. As soon as Uncle Owen turned up, I was ready.

'What time did you get up today, Squirt?' he asked.

'Seven-thirty.'

I watched over his shoulder, eyes glued to every move he made as if my life depended on it. Maybe it did. When he hit ALARM SET

I noticed a small 22 AUG in the corner of the display.

'And what time do you have to get up tomorrow?'

'Seven-fifteen!' I blurted.

Mum glanced at me from the sink but she didn't say anything.

'Alrighty.' Uncle Owen stabbed away and a small 23 AUG lit up – tomorrow's date. 'Oh yeah ... I almost forgot.' He pushed another button. RECUR lit up on the display and the date disappeared. 'Push that so the alarm goes off on recurring Wednesdays, okay, Squirt? Otherwise it'll just go off tomorrow and you'll have to set it again next Wednesday.'

'Alright, thanks, Uncle Owen,' I said quickly. *Very interesting*. Up until now the alarm had been set for today's date and no other. Was that why I'd been stuck in the same day over and over?

The rest of the day was ... well, the same as the day before. It was eerie and weird and even a little bit lonely – stuff happened around me that I'd seen before and I couldn't talk to anyone about it. For everyone else, life was completely normal.

At least the maths test was a piece of cake, because we'd gone through all the answers in class after the test on Tuesday Take Two. So by Tuesday Take Three, I was able to do it all the right way. I even showed the working-out properly.

I didn't really think much of it until Mrs O'Connor came over to say well done.

'You've improved so much, Sam,' she said. 'On the test two weeks ago you only managed fifty-three per cent, so to make a hundred today is a real improvement. It just shows what you can do if you put your mind to it. Yes?'

'Yeah, I guess,' I said. Teachers were always telling me dumb stuff like that.

Not that I'd mind making it to another maths test. The way things were going, I wasn't even sure I'd make it to Wednesday. I still had four long days until my birthday!

When I got home, I went straight for the clock. Something about the new setting was making me nervous. If the clock really was causing all the drama, I didn't want to take any chances and set it wrong.

I thought I was pretty clear on how it all worked. I hit ALARM SET and cleared the alarm for Tuesday altogether. Then I cleared the RECUR setting for Wednesday's alarm. When I'd finished, the alarm was set for 7:15 on WED 23 AUG – just that date, and no other.

I wasn't sure what to hope for. I definitely didn't want to keep living through Tuesday over and over. But to wake up on Wednesday after changing the clock like I just had . . . well, that would freak me out for a whole new reason.

It would mean that Uncle Owen's clock was a time machine.

As soon as I woke up, I knew it was Wednesday. For a start, the new birthday clock stood beside my bed, just where I'd left it.

The display said 07:15 WED with a small 23 AUG in the corner. Thank goodness! *Hello, Wednesday. Here I am, at last . . .*

I picked up the clock. Wow. How awesomely amazing was this! My very own time machine.

It hadn't been any fun getting stuck in a series of Tuesdays, but now that I knew how the clock worked . . .

I licked my lips.

I sure didn't want to get stuck on a series of Wednesdays, so I hit ALARM SET and chose the next day's date: 07:30 THUR 24 AUG. I put the clock down.

The pale green display glowed steadily. All that power. At my fingertips. Just waiting for me to push the button.

I picked up the clock again. For a moment, my finger hovered over the ALARM SET button.

I pushed it: 07:30 FRI 25 AUG.

I held my breath, and pushed one more time to reach 07:30 SAT 26 AUG. My birthday. I half-expected the clock to explode, or the world to go into a time warp. But the clock just kept humming faintly with the alarm set on my birthday . . .

When it was time for bed, I double-checked the alarm setting. Maybe it wouldn't even work. For all I knew it might not be possible to travel into the future. Somehow, going back a day made more sense than travelling to a time that hadn't happened yet.

I put the clock beside my bed and lay down, staring at the pale green glow. In the morning, I'd find out.

Slowly I became aware of things around me – the warmth of my pillow, shrill tweets from outside my window. Even before I opened my eyes I sensed more light in my room than usual.

That was because the blind was up. Strange. The blind had been down when I went to sleep.

Then I realised. If today was Saturday then anything could have happened in the two days since I went to sleep.

My heart raced as I sat up. Could it have worked? Could today be my birthday?

Feeling a whole lot excited and a little bit nervous, I tiptoed up the hall. I wasn't sure why.

Tiptoeing just seemed the right thing for a time traveller to do.

I peeked into the kitchen, and for a moment thought that maybe I'd whizzed back three years to when Dad still lived with us. There he was, sitting at the table with his back to me and sipping from a coffee cup.

Maybe he'd dropped round early for my birthday . . .

'Dad!' I cried.

The cup clattered to the table, a brown puddle spilling from it. Dad didn't stop to clean it up. He turned in his seat and gasped. Then with one great spring he was out of the chair and hugging me.

Wow. Birthdays always make me feel loved.

Dad pulled out of the hug and cupped my face in his rough hands, looking into my eyes as if checking for clues to some mystery.

'Rachel!' he called, still peering at me. His voice was croaky, as if he'd stayed up late the night before.

Maybe he had been up late, because Mum appeared looking as if she'd slept in her clothes. The skin under her eyes was dark and baggy.

When she saw me she froze. Then her whole body quivered and she burst out crying, rushed to me and pressed my face into her shaking chest. I'd never seen Mum like that before.

It was around about then that I realised I'd made a huge mistake.

'Where have you been?' Dad asked.

Mum pulled out of the hug for a moment, as if checking it really was me, then grabbed me into her arms again.

I wasn't sure what to say. Not that it was even easy to breathe let alone talk with the way Mum was squeezing my head.

Where *had* I been? It was an eerie feeling, now that I thought about it properly. My parents had been here, wondering where I was, while I'd been *nowhere*. Travelling straight from Wednesday . . . Slipping through time.

I'd been so keen to use the clock to get to my birthday that I hadn't thought what it would be like for the people left to live through Thursday and Friday without me.

'I'm sorry,' I said into Mum's shoulder. 'I didn't realise . . . See, I went to sleep and I just—'

'He must have been drugged,' Dad said over the top of me. 'I'll call the police.'

'No! No, call the hospital first,' said Mum.

Dad went for the phone while Mum made me lie down. What a great birthday.

It turned into the longest day of my life, but not in a good way. A doctor came, took samples of my blood and took them away for tests, then a special policewoman came to interview me. I went along with it all, telling them I was fine. I'd just gone to sleep and then woken up on Saturday. Not that anyone believed me.

Through it all, I couldn't stop looking at Mum. I could see from the tightness around her eyes that she was living through her worst nightmare. It didn't seem to matter that I was safe. Something about her had changed.

When I finally made it to the end of the

day, I couldn't set the alarm fast enough. Back to the Thursday that I'd skipped past: 24 AUG. I double- and triple-checked that I'd set it right then gently placed the clock back in its spot. I didn't want anything to go wrong with the trip backwards in time.

Tomorrow ... well, *last Thursday* really, it would be as if the nightmare had never happened.

It wasn't until then that I started to imagine all the other things that could have gone wrong with travelling into the future. What would have happened if I'd skipped ahead more than two days ... like years ahead, to ... I don't know ... 2095?

What if everyone had been vaccinated against some new disease that killed me as soon as I woke up? What if there had been a nuclear war and everything was radioactive? What if they'd built an airport where my house was and I got squashed!

Anything could be waiting for me in the future. Until I got there, how would I know?

When I woke up on Thursday morning, the first thing I did was look for Mum. She was in her bedroom, head tilted forwards so she could brush the back of her hair.

I smiled. It was so good to see her . . . well, see the back of her head anyway. 'Hey, Mum! What's the date today?'

'Date?' She flipped back her hair, and smiled the way she used to smile. The strange look in her eyes was gone.

'Well . . .' She began brushing again. 'It's two days before your birthday, Sam. Thursday the twenty-fourth.'

I wanted to grab her in a hug, but I just said, 'Thanks, Mum!' and headed back to my room. Everything was back to normal. Almost.

I switched off the clock, pulled out the batteries and crammed everything into my sock drawer. I had to pull out a few socks to make room.

No more time travel for me. Going back into the past was boring and sort of lonely. Going into the future was downright dangerous.

I slid the drawer shut and brushed my hands.

If only I'd left it there.

6

On Monday after maths, Mrs O'Connor called me over to her desk. I took my time, still floating on the memory of a weekend of surf.

My birthday, second time round, had turned out to be really good. Mum and Dad gave me a surfboard, though I was pretty sure Uncle Owen had helped choose it. It was a real beauty. So I spent the whole weekend down at The Point, catching waves with my two best friends. The conditions were pretty close to perfect. Now, *that's* what I call a good birthday.

'I've been looking over your marks for the year.' Mrs O'Connor peered at her laptop as she spoke. 'They're a bit up and down, Sam. Do you know why that might be?'

I shrugged, though I did have an idea. My marks in maths were probably the exact opposite to the weather. Good weather the afternoon before a test meant time at the beach, and a bad mark in maths. That was, unless I'd seen the test already somehow . . .

Mrs O'Connor leaned back in her chair. 'You know, Sam, you're a smart kid . . .' She trailed off and sighed. For a moment she just looked at me. 'You remind me of your Uncle Owen, actually. I taught him too. Smart as a tack, but not willing to apply himself.'

I grinned and nodded, feeling proud. 'Yeah, he's really smart.' Even Uncle Owen didn't know just how smart he actually was.

Mrs O'Connor smiled. 'Just promise me you'll keep working, okay? That hundred per cent last week has really bumped up your average. It's a pity you did so badly in the test before last. If it wasn't for that, you'd be averaging over eighty.'

'Alright, I promise. Thanks,' I said, and walked out to lunch feeling weird and a bit of a fraud. I knew I'd sort of, by accident, *cheated* on the last test, but at least after going over it I really had understood the maths properly.

The way Mrs O'Connor had been speaking made me feel . . . I don't know . . . it made me feel as if I really *did* have brains; as if I was a kid with a bright future. It made me want to work a bit harder at least.

My uncle was, after all, the inventor of a time machine. Who knew what I could do if I tried? Maybe I could be one of those people who *did things*. And I was a bit disappointed about my mark in maths. I could be averaging over eighty? If only I'd put in a bit of effort the test before last . . .

When I got home, I pulled the clock out of the drawer and stared at it.

I sure didn't want to risk going into the future again. But going into the past hadn't been all *that* bad. What if I went back two and a bit weeks to the test I'd messed up? It wasn't as if anyone would think I'd disappeared. What could it hurt?

The biggest downside that I could see to the whole idea would be having to live without a surfboard all over again. But at least I knew I was going to get one for my birthday. And it kind of seemed like a smart plan, an investment in my own future. A chance to really be the bright kid Mrs O'Connor thought I was.

Carefully I slid the batteries in and pushed the button, smiling as the clock hummed back to life. For a few seconds, the humming increased as I guess it checked our location by GPS and set itself at the correct time. It was pretty cool to see it working again.

I tapped the ALARM SET button gently with the tip of my finger. Then I took a breath and cycled through all the days of the month until I came to TUE 8 AUG, the day of our last maths test.

I'd finally worked out how to use the time machine properly. Not for skipping boring bits of life, but for fixing things I'd messed up, like sprained ankles and maths test. There didn't seem any harm in using it for that.

I left the clock beside my bed and grabbed my surfboard. One last surf, before I slipped back in time.

It was the strangest feeling, waking up two and a bit weeks in the past. It was more disconcerting than just going back a day. I'd been here before, and yet I couldn't remember much. It all just seemed so . . . freakishly normal.

The first thing that spooked me was rolling over to find that my new clock was gone. Then I realised of course it wouldn't be there. This was two weeks before Uncle Owen had given it to me.

Okay. I just had to wait until Uncle Owen turned up on the Tuesday morning before my birthday. I'd been through that morning enough times to know exactly what was going to happen. He'd have it wrapped in creased, white tissue paper, with a crooked bit of sticky tape . . .

I grabbed a piece of toast and an OJ. Then I hit the books. Even though I was two weeks in the past, I felt somehow fresh and new. Here I was, doing things the way they should have been done. I was still me, but a new improved version. Sam Take Two.

I couldn't remember the maths test very well but I knew what kinds of sums were on it. I looked over the stuff we'd been doing in class and even found one problem that I was pretty certain I remembered from the test. So I made sure I knew that problem back-to-front as well as how to do the others.

Even before we got our marks back, I knew I'd done well. This time round I understood the maths properly, so I knew I'd answered most of them right.

'Well done, Sam,' said Mrs O'Connor as she handed back my test sheet.

'Thanks.' I was really pleased with my 92.5 per cent. It wasn't a hundred, but it was pretty close.

The way Mrs O'Connor smiled at me then made me sure my plan was worth it.

After that, it was all just a matter of . . . well, *living* through the next two weeks. I was surprised how much stuff I'd forgotten. Sometimes I felt a bit of déjà vu but most of the time it was no different from normal life. After all, so many days are more or less the same as the day before. Get up. Go to school. Come home. For those two weeks, everything was pretty much life as usual, except with a couple of bad bits removed.

At one point I remembered cutting myself as

I sliced through an orange. I could make sure that didn't happen second time round. And I remembered being caught in a freak storm at the park one Saturday. So that was easy to avoid.

Another time Uncle Owen phoned to ask what I wanted for my birthday.

'A clock!' I said straight away. 'You know, with an alarm that you can set for a different time each day of the week?' I sure didn't want to miss out on that present. Even though it had taken me a while how to work out how to use it properly, it was still the best gift I'd ever been given.

When finally I made it to the Tuesday before my birthday (for the *fourth* time), I was really excited. This time I was going to say a proper thanks to Uncle Owen for giving me such a great present. After all I was the new, improved Sam now.

I was dressed, fed and all ready to go when I heard the familiar click and creak of the back door opening.

'Happy birthday, Squirt!'

'Thanks, Uncle Owen, this is great!' I smiled and took the package. It seemed to have been wrapped a bit neater this time, but he had still used the same creased, white tissue paper.

'Do you want a quick coffee?' asked Mum.

'Nah thanks, Sis.'

I tore the wrapping away to find . . .

A box?

'But . . .' This wasn't right. The box showed a picture of a clock radio and bullet points listing all the things it could do. I didn't need to check whether time travel was one. 'Hang on.' I flipped the lid, hoping to find wires looped everywhere and buttons on the side.

But inside the box was a normal alarm clock that had come from a shop. It was neat, stylish and just that. A clock.

'But . . . how . . .' I spluttered. 'I mean . . . You're meant to *make* a clock.'

For a moment Uncle Owen stared at me. Then

he raised his eyebrows and nodded. 'Funny you should say that, Squirt, because I've been tinkering with an old clock for a while. But then you asked for one and I started thinking about what kind of clock you had in mind . . . so I decided to go shopping.'

Shopping! I couldn't believe it.

'What? Don't you like it?' asked Uncle Owen. 'She's a beauty.'

I could feel Mum frowning at me: *remember your manners.* But I was too time-travel-looped-out to worry about that. Somehow, by asking for a clock and not a surfboard, I'd set Uncle Owen on a train of thought that had stopped him from making my present . . . that had stopped him from *making my time machine.*

'So, you're still tinkering with the clock at home, aren't you?' I asked.

'Yeah, well,' Owen sighed. 'No. Not really. Once I saw all the clocks at the shop, there didn't seem much point. It's amazing all the things that clocks can do these days.' He shrugged. 'If you don't like this one we can swap it. Anything you want a clock to do, Squirt, we'll be able to buy it.'

If only he knew! I thought quickly. 'I was hoping . . . maybe . . . you could keep working on the one you were making,' I said. 'It would be good to have one that can check conditions at The Point . . . you know, with an alarm that goes off when the surf is good.'

Again, Owen stared at me, head tilted in surprise. Then his face broke into a massive grin. 'Hey, great minds think alike! I've thought of that too. But I'm not sure it's even possible, Squirt. I'd have to find a way to make it read the data at the weather station . . .' He shrugged and stood up.

'You can do it, Uncle Owen. I *know* you can.'

'Maybe one day,' he said and ruffled my hair.

This was a disaster. I wasn't sure what else to say.

'Have a good one on Saturday, Squirt,' he said. 'Sorry again that I can't make it.'

'Nah, that's okay. Thanks,' I said.

I watched him walk away, swallowing down a lump in my throat. Not from sadness exactly, more from frustration.

And extreme disappointment.

That was two years ago. We still don't have a time machine.

Last year, I managed to talk Uncle Owen into making another clock, and I even helped him. I learnt a heap about electronics and programming. But even though the new clock looked the same, it didn't work like the old one. I don't know why. Maybe there was a piece missing. Or maybe, the first time round, Uncle Owen had had trouble programming it the way he wanted and thought up a creative solution that didn't happen this time. I've done my head in thinking about it.

When I tried explaining to Uncle Owen what had happened he thought I was totally loopy, talking about a time machine that didn't exist.

'Time travel just isn't possible, Squirt,' he kept saying. 'Not the way you're describing it.'

Fair enough. Unless he'd seen the time machine work, he had no reason to believe it was possible.

I've given up on Uncle Owen's clock, but I haven't given up completely. I still don't know how the time travel worked, but I lived through it so I *know* it's possible. The missing piece or the creative solution ... I know it's out there, somewhere. And I'm going to find it.

I still go surfing, mostly on weekends. It helps me think. But I work really hard at school too. Mrs O'Connor can hardly believe it. I'm going to get good grades, then go to uni and learn as much as I can. Maybe I'll never work out the secret to time travel, but I'm going to give it my best shot. I'll spend my whole life trying if I need to.

Even though it doesn't exist anymore, that time machine completely changed my future.

IT BEGAN WITH A TINGLE

1

I FIRST REALISED something strange was happening when the back of my arm began to tingle.

It was just one lump, about the size of a mosquito bite, halfway between my shoulder and my elbow. It didn't feel sore or itchy the way a bite might feel, it tingled and was weirdly warm . . .

Maybe it will just go away, I thought, and chose a top with long sleeves to wear.

I had to wear a long-sleeved top the next day, too.

And the next.

For the rest of the week I wore long sleeves, because the lump on my arm didn't go away. It grew bigger.

Whenever I had a moment alone, I rubbed my finger over the lump. Not because it hurt, but because it felt *interesting* to touch, like getting to know a fresh scar that stretches in weird ways when I move the skin.

Soon the lump stuck out from my arm the way a cheek does when a tongue pushes from the other side.

I was rubbing a finger over my windcheater at the bus stop when my friend Zoe frowned at me.

'What are you doing?' she asked.

'Ah . . . nothing,' I said, dropping my hand. Then I changed my mind. 'Do you want to see something weird?' I rolled up my sleeve.

'Brooke!' Zoe cried. 'What *is* that?'

She peered close, frowning and tilting her head.

'I don't know,' I said, peering over my shoulder trying to get a better look. 'It just . . . started growing.'

'Eww!' said Zoe, and stepped back. 'You should take that thing to a doctor.'

I pulled down my sleeve. 'You think?'

Zoe nodded.

But I didn't show the lump to a doctor. After that, I didn't show it to anyone. I knew it looked weird, but I didn't mind how it looked. I was fascinated by the way it *felt*. It wasn't numb or sore. It was tingly in the mornings and warm at night. If I hadn't known better, I would have sworn I could feel different parts forming inside it, like muscle and bone.

I was right.

Two weeks after the lump started to grow, I found that I could make it move. I had to use a mirror at first, looking over my shoulder and back-to-front. If I stared at the lump and concentrated hard, I was able to make it wiggle – *up and down, side to side, round and round and round.* It was a bit like trying to make my ears wiggle, but so much better . . .

Each time it worked I laughed in amazement. It looked like a short fat finger waving hello from the back of my arm. The lump had to be connected to my brain somehow. Whatever it was, it was part of *me*.

That's a pretty big thing to find out. It was like the time when Squeak, our guinea pig, had babies and we didn't even know she was pregnant. Something alive had come from . . . nowhere.

I thought about showing my mum. *Hey, Mum, look what I can do!* But then I imagined what she would say next. *I'll book you in to see the doctor, Brooke.*

Somehow I didn't want a doctor peering and poking at my lump. I didn't want to think about the way a doctor would look at *me*.

So I spent more and more time alone in my room. Moving the lump became a bit of an obsession. I especially loved making it move inside my red windcheater, rubbing it soothingly against the soft fabric fuzz.

Soon the lump had grown so big it was difficult to hide. My right arm bulged underneath my baggy school shirt. It was fat now, and long. It looked like two sausages stuck side by side on the back of my arm. I could feel the hard bone beneath the skin of one sausage, then thin flesh connecting them, before the bone in the other sausage.

Then, four weeks after it first appeared, it stopped growing.

Over a few days, the fleshy strip between the two sausages became thinner and thinner until it was paper-thin and dry.

Then, four or five weeks after I first felt the tingle, I woke up in the middle of the night.

Groggily, I rubbed my sausage lumps. As I opened my eyes a raw kind of desperation came over me. I'd never felt anything like it. Absolutely nothing was going to stop me from scratching my lumps. This was the mother of all itches.

I switched on my lamp, grabbed a ruler, and started to rub like there was no tomorrow. Flakes of skin fell away like huge bits of puff pastry. Monster-sized dandruff.

For a while I kept rubbing, soothing, scratching . . .

Then something amazing happened

The two sausage parts *split apart,* everywhere except the very end. Slowly I was able to stretch it out – an arm with a hinge of an elbow.

The movement felt new and natural at the same time.

I lifted it and rubbed the last flakes of dry skin. They fell away to show stubby lumps on the end.

Five of them.

2

It was the most amazing thing.

Slowly in the lamplight I came to understand what I was seeing. I reached out and touched, felt it *respond*, realised that *I* was being touched. I ran my hand along my new right arm, then my old right arm, comparing them, looking for difference. Other than size they were the same. Even the fingers of my new hand were complete with knuckles and tiny fingernails.

At first, I couldn't move the new arm very well. If I tried to do something, my normal right arm moved instead. To get the new arm working, I found I had to move both in tandem

– big-arm and baby-arm dancing together. But slowly as the night hours passed, I learnt how to make my new arm move to my command – straightening it out and twirling the hand, playing air-piano with stubby fingers. For those first few hours it was just me and my new arm, hidden by the cloak of night.

The next morning I bandaged my two right arms together, mostly to hide the new one, but also as a reminder not to move it. I was surprised when no one noticed that anything was different; the whole world had changed as far as I was concerned. I'd gone to sleep the old me then woken to find I was *different* … a different version of me.

Of course, I knew what people would say if they saw my new arm. *Ugly, awful, freaky, weird* … But I didn't feel the same. This arm had grown from my body. It was part of me.

As the days slipped past, I became used to keeping it still during the day then coming home and enjoying the relief of being able to stretch and be free. I said no to a couple of things on the weekend and some days I pretended to be sick so that I could stay home from school, but most of the time everything was surprisingly normal. I saw my friends at school and kept up with them online from home, same as always.

Even though my new arm was still a bit weak, I began using it whenever I was alone. It was in exactly the right spot for moving the mouse, keeping my other two hands free for typing. I wasn't coordinated enough to do things like write with it, but I was good enough to move the arrow where I wanted. Double-click here. Right-click there. Sometimes I just held an apple in my new hand, munching while I typed. After a while, working on the computer with my new arm became so natural that I found it hard to remember what it had been like working with just two hands.

I was chatting online when I received an event invitation. *Cool.* I clicked straight through.

Zoe Whelan has invited you to her Birthday Party.
Event: Zoe's birthday party
Where: Harrington Leisure Centre

Start time: 2.30pm, Saturday 26 October
Bring: your swimmers!

A pool party? I sighed and looked at my baby hand, resting on the mouse. Could I go? Maybe I could tell everyone that I had a sore arm . . . *I can come, but I can't swim.*

But that would be a disaster. People would ask questions. What if they wanted to *look* at my sore arm . . .

I sighed again, and clicked decline.

Seconds later a message from Zoe appeared: 'What the ???'

'Soz,' I replied. 'I'm busy.'

'BUSY???' sent back Zoe. 'How can you be busy?'

I turned away from the screen, wondering what I could say. Then I turned back just long enough to log off.

The next day I stayed home from school, even though Mum raised her eyebrows and said, '*Really...*' when I said I was sick.

To be honest, I did feel sick. Sick with fear. The weather was getting warmer; it was only a matter of time before someone asked why I never wore short sleeves.

When Mum came home from work, I was sitting on the couch.

She pulled off her coat and hung it up. 'Hey Brooke. How're you feeling?'

'There's something's you need to see.' Slowly, I slipped my jacket off my shoulders and let it fall behind me on the couch. Time seemed to slow down as Mum's lips parted. The only sound was an intake of breath. Everything else about her was frozen in shock.

'Oh, Brooke . . .' Mum whispered. She lifted my jacket from the couch and draped it over my new arm, covering it up again. She hugged me, hand at the top of my back, chest close, not touching me below the shoulders.

After a while she pulled back, holding my face in her hands. 'Brooke . . . you poor thing . . . How long have you been hiding this?'

I shook my head, tears welling now that I could see myself through her eyes. I'll never forget the way she was looking at me – so tender, so ready to fix everything. But there was something else in there too.

It made me wonder what it must be like to find out your daughter is a freak.

3

The next few days were a blur. So many waiting rooms. So many X-rays and tests. Mum spent half her time filling out forms and the other half on the phone. At one point we drove an hour and a half across the city, only to be told by a doctor that his specialty was conjoined twins, not my 'situation'. And there was no mention of me going back to school.

Some things weren't so bad, though. Now that I'd shown Mum my new arm, I didn't have to hide it anymore. It felt so good leaving it free to move naturally – to grow strong and, I don't know, integrate . . . become a part of who I was.

I was deliberately avoiding the internet and the phone. So there wasn't much to do when we were at home.

One afternoon, for something to do, I made a cake. Mum watched with her ear to the phone, on hold with another doctor, as I poured the thick batter into a cake pan. I held the bowl in two hands and used my third to scrape with a spoon. As I worked I glanced up, anxious to see if she had realised how *useful* my new arm could be. But she had turned away.

For a few nights I shook salt onto my dinner while still holding my knife and fork. Not because the food needed it really, but just because I could. Each time, Mum kept talking or eating as if she hadn't noticed – as if my third arm wasn't even there.

I knew her better than that, though.

Once when I poked my head into the study, her shoulders jerked and she rushed to close the file she was working on.

'What are you doing?' I asked.

'Oh . . . just writing my diary,' she said, her voice pitched slightly higher than normal.

The next time she was out shopping I snuck into the study and booted up her computer. It was password protected but that didn't stop me for long. The password was her birthday then mine. I mean, honestly – she was so predictable.

Most of Mum's diary was a log of all the specialists we'd seen and all the stuff they'd said. But underneath all that was paragraph after paragraph of typing, an outpouring of Mum's thoughts.

How could this happen? it began. *Did I do something wrong when I was pregnant?*

What if someone discovers what's happened? A kid at school? A parent? What if they went to the media? They'd have a field day with something like this. I can't stand to think how they'd treat her. The awful things they'd say. I'm scared we're on the edge of disaster. Something like this could affect the rest of her life.

If this gets out, I'm scared I won't be able to protect her anymore.

I shut down the computer after that. Reading Mum's diary made me feel like a freak all over again. No wonder she couldn't stand to look at my new arm. All she saw were the ways it might make my life worse.

My new arm was something amazing for me, but something entirely different for Mum.

Later that week, Mum was over the moon because we were referred to see a doctor whose name had been mentioned a couple of times already. He was a specialist at the children's hospital – Dr Alexander Drew.

Dr Drew was different right from the start – efficient and confident, jolly even. He acted as if he dealt with this kind of thing all the time.

'Don't worry, Ms Miskin,' he said, smiling at us from across a huge desk. 'We'll have your daughter fixed up in a jiffy.' He smiled reassuringly. 'It's quite fascinating, really. Just the human body throwing up a random mutation. Nothing to worry about at all.'

Mum seemed to grow in her chair like a flower. She smiled as she listened, nodding here and there rather than asking questions as she usually did.

Soon the discussion moved to things like admittance forms and operation procedures.

'I'm expecting a fast recovery time,' said Dr Drew. 'This is a straightforward procedure.'

That's when it hit me. This man was going to cut off my new arm. *Of course he was. What else had I been expecting?*

As Dr Drew's voice faded into the background, a cold space settled in me. My new arm was a mutation . . . but it was also part of me. I tried to imagine how I'd feel once it was gone. Not the same as before, I knew that already. It would be as if something was missing.

But I had to get used to the idea of not having it around. Without my new arm, everything would go back to normal.

Mum would look at me again.

The next day, Mum and I were back at the hospital. But this time I was clutching a bag of clothes and my favourite electronic game. I had three days of tests booked in and no date yet for the operation.

When we stepped out of the lift on the top floor there didn't seem to be any signs for

Ward 5G. Eventually a nurse noticed us looking lost. She stared at me curiously when Mum told her which ward we were looking for, but she didn't say anything. She led the way to a door with no sign on it, punched a code into a small keypad and ushered us through.

Inside, it was still and quiet. The walls were sky blue.

As we walked up to the nurses' station, movement on a computer monitor behind the desk caught my eye. A strange feeling came over me as I recognised myself standing next to Mum. The ward obviously had a whole closed circuit TV network hooked up through its computers. I checked for the camera, and found it high up in the corner above the door. Mum handed over a few more forms, and another nurse showed me to my room.

'Well, isn't this lovely?' said Mum once the nurse had gone. She pushed down on the bed a couple of times, as if we'd just checked into a hotel.

But I wasn't looking at *my* bed; I was looking at the three other beds in the room. One was clearly empty, but the two others had bedding, get-well cards on the bedside table and clipboards at the end . . .

I wasn't the only one.

Mum wanted to stay and help me unpack, but I told her not to hang around.

There wasn't anything scheduled for the rest of the day and I knew she'd be back in the morning for the next round of tests.

'Don't worry. I'll be fine.'

For a moment Mum frowned at me. Then she nodded. 'Alright,' she said. 'But call me whenever you want. I don't mind what time.'

'Okay, thanks.' A quick hug, then she was gone.

I looked around. One of the beds had a soft floppy elephant on the pillow and fairy cards everywhere. The other bed was more of mystery.

Someone was definitely using it, but there was nothing to show how old they were.

For something to do, I checked out the bathroom. No surprises there. Then, feeling self-conscious, I poked my head into the hall. No one was at the nurses' station. I could hear faint canned laughter.

I followed the sound past a door with another keypad and to a room signed COMMON ROOM. It was painted bright yellow and had shelves stacked with books and board games. An episode of *Get Smart* was on the TV.

'Hello. What's your name?' said a little girl, standing up from the rug. She was only about as tall as a toddler, but her face made her look six or seven.

'Hi, I'm Brooke,' I said, and stepped forward so I could see what she was doing. Puzzle pieces were strewn around her feet. It was obvious straight away why she was here – she had a huge lump at the top of her back.

She was a hunchback. *Poor thing . . .*

'I'm Erin, and that's Jack,' she said, pointing at the back of an armchair that was facing the TV.

Feeling nervous, I stepped around the armchair. What was I going to find?

A boy about my age turned and looked me up and down. For a moment his eyes stopped on the bulge of my sleeve. 'Hi,' he mumbled before turning back to the TV.

'Hi,' I said, trying to look him over without being too obvious. He was wearing a baseball cap and seemed completely normal.

Erin tugged at my sleeve. 'Do you believe in fairies?' she whispered.

'Ah . . .' I wasn't sure how to answer that.

'Because I can show you for real,' she cried. 'Look!'

The next thing I knew, Erin was pulling off her windcheater. Underneath she was wearing a tank top . . .

I gasped and stepped back.

Between Erin's shoulderblades was a folded pair of wings. They weren't sparkly and colourful like fairy wings. I could see thin fingers of bone inside a fleshy membrane.

'See? It's me! I'm a real live fairy!' she chanted, jumping up and down.

I swallowed. Other than their flesh-pink colour, they looked like the wings of a bat. A wave of nausea washed through me. I was repulsed, but at the same time I couldn't look away. Was this how Mum had felt when she first saw my arm?

'Can you fly?' I managed.

Erin stopped jumping, and pouted. 'No,' she said. For a moment I thought she was going to cry, then I realised she was concentrating, holding her breath.

Slowly the wings unfolded. They were wider than I'd realised. Networks of blue veins stretched beneath the skin.

I opened my mouth, searching for something to say.

Erin breathed out in a rush. 'I can't even flap them. Dr Drew says he needs to cut them off because I'm not growing like other kids. But I don't mind being small. *Really*. Fairies are meant to be small. Are you going to get something cut off your arm?'

Now I was speechless for another reason. I hadn't even noticed her looking at my arm.

'Yes,' I said, pulling off my jacket so that Erin could see. 'I am.'

For the first time I started to feel glad to have found Dr Drew. I didn't want to live my life with people thinking the things about me that I'd just thought about Erin.

After a close inspection, Erin looked up at me. 'Dr Drew's a good doctor, isn't he?' she said.

'Yeah, we're lucky to be here, I reckon.' As I spoke, something made me look at Jack's armchair. He was scowling around the backrest at me.

When he saw me glance over, he disappeared from view.

So I sat down on the floor next to Erin and settled in to watch *Get Smart*.

A bit later, Erin's mum turned up and stayed while we settled in for the night. It was nice to have someone's mum around, not that I was homesick exactly. The nurses were friendly enough.

I didn't think I was going to sleep very well in the ward, but I must have because later that night, something woke me up. It was Jack, shaking my shoulder.

I opened my eyes and yawned.

'Want to see something?' he asked.

5

In bare feet we slipped across to the common room. A radio was playing faintly in the nurses' station, but no one noticed we were up.

Without a word, Jack pulled off his cap and turned his back to me.

I rubbed my face, wondering groggily why he still wore that cap at night. He was staring at the wall. *Strange guy.*

Then the creepiest sensation came over me. It was like when you realise someone is watching you, but you're not sure how you know. Then you turn to see, and there really *is* someone watching you . . .

That was because I *was* being watched, by an eye in the back of Jack's head. It was a light-brown eye complete with eyelashes and eyebrow, peering out from a bald patch at the back of his head. It was the most unnerving thing.

When the eye blinked, I gasped and covered my mouth with a hand. 'Can you see me?' I asked, even though I knew the answer. That eye was focused, staring right at me. I wanted to turn away.

'Sure,' said Jack to the wall. 'Go on, hold up some fingers. Everyone wants to.'

Slowly, I raised my hand, holding up three fingers. 'Wait, hold on,' I said. Spreading them as wide as I could, I held up four fingers of my new hand, plus two on each of my others.

Jack snorted. 'Two plus two, plus four makes eight. Very funny.'

He hooked his cap back on his head, and turned to face me. When our eyes met, I knew we were thinking the same thing. No one else in the world could have done what we just did.

'So how . . .' I started. 'I mean, I don't get . . .'

'I'm not very good at seeing in three-sixty degrees. It's hard and disorienting,' he said. 'I see behind me best when I have my other eyes closed.' He glanced out the door, then back to me.

'Or if I flick my focus: in front, behind, in front, behind. To be honest, I use it most at night. When I'm sleeping, my third eye can take stuff in.'

I nodded, not sure what to say. A new arm was pretty useful, but a new eye was out of this world.

'Anyway,' said Jack and adjusted his cap. 'Come on. Follow me.'

It wasn't until he was pushing numbers on a keypad at the end of the hall that I realised Jack's eye wasn't the reason he'd woken me. There was something else he wanted me to see.

The door clicked and swung open. Jack grinned.

'We're not meant to be doing this, are we?' I said evenly.

He shrugged. 'Being a freak has got to have some benefits, don't you think?'

I looked past him into the darkness, unsure.

'Are you coming in or not?'

I nodded.

Quietly Jack shut the door behind me and flicked on a light. We were in an office. Big desk, bookshelves, computer, swivel chair . . .

For a moment I thought about jumping on to check if anyone was online, but Jack was already pushing buttons on another lock.

'How did you work out the codes?' I whispered.

'How do you think?' When the second door clicked, Jack pushed it open and switched on another light. 'Turn out that light, will you?'

Switch flicked, I followed him into the next room. It was the most amazing place.

The first thing I noticed was a shelf of jars with *things* floating in them. One looked like a snake, or was it a coiled tail? The next was a fleshy blob. I had no idea what it was. Smaller jars held fingers and toes. Up high, I could see a tiny hand and I wondered if it belonged to an arm somewhere.

Jack was standing next to a light box mounted on the wall. It flickered a bit when he turned it on. Without a word he pulled an X-ray out of a drawer and hooked it up.

I tilted my head, trying to work out what I was looking at, then breathed in. 'That . . . foot's on *backwards* . . .'

'I think it's the knee that's in reverse,' said Jack. 'See how the pelvis is facing that way?'

I nodded, not wanting to look away. But other parts of the room called out for my attention. A noticeboard was covered with all kinds of photos – a foot that looked more like a flipper, a shin with shiny hard skin like scales . . .

Some photos were faded and old, as if they'd been taken in the seventies or eighties.

'Has this been happening, like, all the time?' I breathed.

'They're mostly babies, did you notice?' said Jack. 'They amputate the extra limb before they even make it out of hospital.' He opened a drawer, put back the X-ray and pulled another out. The fact that he knew where everything was made me think he'd spent a lot of time in here.

'It's just . . .' I shook my head, looking down so that I could think for a bit. All these parts used to *belong* to someone . . . a kid who was out there in the world. What kind of life did they lead now?

The next X-ray showed a small shoulder, I think, with bone sticking out. It made me think of Erin and her wings, though this looked different.

'Have you found any . . . eyes?' I asked.

Jack looked away. 'No,' he said to the wall. Muscles clenched in his jaw. 'I've looked through this whole room four times and never found a single eye.'

He put the last X-ray back in the drawer, and switched off the light box.

In silence, we made our way back outside. Without needing to be asked, I switched on the light in the office before Jack locked up the room.

The hall was quiet, empty and dark.

'Thanks,' I whispered, even though it seemed like a weird thing to say.

Jack responded with another shrug.

We tiptoed back down the hall and into our beds. It felt wrong not being able to talk about it all, but at the same time I wasn't sure what I would have said.

I didn't sleep very well for the rest of the night. I couldn't stop thinking about those babies and kids. How did they feel after their operation? Where were they now? For all I knew, I could have been going to school with one of them.

Once they'd been *fixed*, how could you tell?

The next morning I was woken by the feeling of my blanket being lifted and the mattress moving slightly.

I opened my eyes to see a face duck under the covers.

'Hi, Erin,' I whispered.

The shape giggled before Erin's face appeared. 'It's six forty-seven,' she whispered, holding her wrist about two centimetres from my eyes.

I went cross-eyed trying to focus. 'Not anymore.'

The wrist disappeared. Erin mouthed some words at her watch before saying, 'Six forty-nine.'

'What time does your mum get here?'

'Eight o'clock.'

I yawned. 'Well, that's plenty of time.'

Erin was lying on her side and I could see the point of a wing over her shoulder. 'I had the most *won*derful dream.'

'What did you dream?'

'I dreamt that I could fly,' she said.

'Tell me all about it,' I said softly.

She snuggled closer. Her feet were cold but the rest of her was toasty. 'I'm running really fast. On top of a hill, or . . . it's like I'm on top of the world. Then all of a sudden there's no more ground, but I'm not scared. I just open my wings and it's so easy. I'm so high . . .' She sighed. 'I just . . . fly.'

I shifted a little to look at her. All I could see was the top of her head. 'So you're not flapping like a bird . . . you're gliding?'

'Is that what it's called?'

I chewed on my bottom lip, thinking. Erin's dream sounded like the hang-gliders I'd seen once when I was bushwalking. Now that I was thinking about it, Erin's wings looked a bit the same when they were open.

I looked at the top of her head again. 'Want to try something before your mum gets here?'

Erin sat up. 'What?'

'Get dressed and I'll meet you in the common room.'

Five minutes later I was pushing everything in the common room against one wall. Erin was trying to help, but was mostly getting in the way.

Jack had followed us, yawning and rubbing his neck, then plonked himself in an armchair.

'You know, we could do with a bit of help,' I panted, straining against a heavy couch.

'Nah. You're doing a great job.'

When everything except for Jack's armchair had been moved, I stood behind the backrest, hooked my fingers under it and tipped . . .

'Alright! Alright!' Jack jumped up and slid his

hands under the front part. Together we lifted it to one side before Jack sat in it again.

'Now, start here, Erin,' I said and went to a corner of the room. There would have been a better run-up in the hall but I didn't want any nurses to see. 'Run as fast as you can until you get here.' I did a slow jog to the centre of the room. 'Then just open your wings and see what happens.'

Erin nodded, her eyes bright.

'On your marks, get set . . . go!'

Fists clenched and face squashed in concentration, Erin trotted to the middle of the room. She did a shallow leap but her wings stayed folded.

She ran back to the end of the room and tried again. This time her wings popped open but by then she'd lost all speed.

'That wasn't very good, was it,' said Erin with a pout.

'No no! It was great!' I nodded encouragingly. 'We're just practising.'

'Maybe she should start with her wings open,' said Jack. He had his leg hooked over the armrest of his chair.

I nodded. 'Okay. Try keeping your wings open the whole way.'

Chest puffed and wings wide, Erin stood in the corner. It was quite a sight.

'Okay, Erin. Ready, set . . . go!'

Her run was completely different this time – more fluid and less up-and-down. Her leap was shallow but she seemed to glide a few centimetres.

'I did it!' she cried, then looked from me to Jack. 'I did, didn't I? I flew a little bit?'

Jack stood up. 'Sure you did! Try again.'

The next time, Erin's leap carried her forwards another half-metre. Not much, but enough for Jack to clap, legs apart like a coach on the sidelines of a football game.

'Lift off!' I yelled.

Erin beamed at me and I grinned back. 'Again?' she asked, though I don't think I could have stopped her if I'd wanted to.

As Erin's leaps carried her further and further, our mood grew brighter until we were cheering and laughing like we were at a party.

We were so deep inside our success that we lost all track of time.

That was, until eight o'clock...

8

'What are you doing?' snapped a voice from the doorway.

It was Erin's mum, hands on hips and eyes narrow. Dr Drew stood next to her on one side and my mum was on the other, hugging a bag and frowning at me. Their mood was the exact opposite of ours. I might have expected that kind of reaction if we'd been caught hanging Erin head first out of a window.

As soon as he realised we were being watched, Jack stepped backwards and adjusted his cap. I hooked my hands together, out of sight and behind my back.

'Mum! Look at me! Look what I can do!' Erin bounded to the corner, wings open and started her run-up.

Erin's mum stepped forward as if to stop her, but Erin was too fast. She ran into a low glide that carried her, feet off the ground, for a good metre and a half.

She landed and turned, jumping and clapping.

'Oh darling . . .' Erin's mum nodded, then turned away, hand over mouth, and shot a look at Dr Drew.

'Now I can keep my wings!' sang Erin.

Mum rushed forward and placed her hands on my shoulders, trying to guide me out of the room. 'Come on, back to the ward.'

'But . . .' I pulled away, confused.

'Come on. This is none of our business,' said Mum, her voice low. 'Oh Brooke, I would have thought you of all people would understand. You shouldn't give Erin false hope.'

Around then I stopped listening to Mum because I'd caught sight of Erin. Her wings were folded and her whole face had crumpled. Wet lines trickled down her red cheeks. Dr Drew and her mum were crouched down to her height.

I felt a rush of anger that was immediately chased by a rush of guilt. I'd been so excited by the idea of teaching her to glide that I hadn't really thought beyond that.

Jack had disappeared somewhere. He wasn't in our room when we got there.

Mum sat on the end of my bed and patted a space next to her, but I sat up near the pillow.

'Listen, Brooke, I know what Erin was doing was exciting. Sure. I get that . . .' She trailed off and sighed. 'I've been talking to Erin's mum. Erin's not growing like she should. It's really best for her to have her wings removed.'

I had my legs crossed on the bed, two hands in my lap, the third resting on my knee.

'Think what it would be like if she kept them,' Mum pushed gently. 'They'd grow too big to hide. She'd be teased at school. Everywhere she went, people would *stare*.'

I kept my head down, looking at my three arms and trying to block out what she was saying. Maybe she was right, but that didn't mean I wanted to hear it.

'Brooke . . . look . . .' Mum checked over her shoulder at Jack's empty bed. 'Think of it this way, Erin's parents are going to do the best thing for her, even if Erin doesn't understand that right now. The thing is, the decision's not up to *her*.'

Mum leaned close as she said the last part, wanting me to look at her. I kept my head down. She was talking about Erin but I knew she was also talking about me.

I know you don't like being here, but you have no choice.

A loud crash from outside the ward made both of us look up. Mum dashed into the hallway. I followed. Another crash came from the common room.

An alarm sounded and two men in white coats flashed past. I heard a fainter thud then a moment of quiet before another thud. It sounded like rocks being thrown against a wall.

When we reached the common room door, Jack was standing beside the bookcase, which was lying face-down on the floor. The books had spilled out across the carpet, making ready ammunition for Jack to pick up and hurl, discus-style, across the room.

The two orderlies who had rushed past were advancing towards Jack. Dr Drew was standing with his arms folded. 'Drop it,' he snapped.

Jack lifted a book in his hand. His face was

almost without expression but his eyes were fierce with defiance.

'Jack, I mean it!'

With his eyes fixed on Dr Drew, Jack leaned back and flung the book. It missed the doctor's head only because he ducked.

'Don't make this worse than it has to be . . .' said one of the orderlies.

'Stay back,' said Mum with a hand on my back. But I pulled away from her. 'Brooke, *stay back*,' she said again, this time holding my shoulders and forcing me to turn.

I was scared so I let her pull me away.

The last thing I saw was Jack backing into a corner.

That was a long day, a dot-to-dot of visits to specialists followed by a talk with Dr Drew. He spoke about physio, diet, the amount of rest I'd need after the operation, and lots more. I barely listened to any of it. He said nothing about Erin learning to glide.

I didn't see Jack until Mum had gone home and I was back in the ward for dinner. Erin had gone out with her mum, and a curtain had been pulled around Jack's bed. Hushed voices made it seem private and secretive in there.

I sipped my tomato soup as quietly as possible, straining to hear what they were saying. There were three voices, I decided, but I couldn't make out any words. I was surprised at how calm they all sounded. Halfway through my rice pudding, the curtains were pushed back with a jerk and Jack's parents emerged. They walked past with straight backs and didn't look my way.

Jack did, just for a moment. Then he lay with his back to me, facing the window, knees pulled up to his chest.

It was raining gently, the streetlights picking up every falling drop. I slipped out of bed, feeling Jack's eye on me, and stepped across the cold floor. For a moment I paused at the foot of his bed then I hitched myself up to sit on it.

'So . . . what was that all about?'

Jack didn't move. 'Do you really need me to spell it out?'

I sighed. Not really. As the day had gone past, I'd realised something was different for me too. Teaching Erin to fly had been about much more than just her.

'Do you have any idea how many kids I've seen come through here?' asked Jack, still without moving. He didn't wait for an answer. 'Seven . . . all around Erin's age. They come in, chuck a tantrum or two, get fixed up, and disappear.'

I stayed quiet, waiting for Jack to keep going.

'You know why I've seen so many?' He glanced at me, then away. 'Dr Drew doesn't know what to do with me. I've been in and out of this place for nearly three years while he works out how to operate . . . they don't want to leave me *brain-damaged.*'

The last two words hung in the air. I needed to wash them away. 'At least he won't do anything until he's sure . . .'

'You think?' Jack sat up. I wasn't used to seeing him without his cap. His pupils were huge. 'Things can go wrong with *any* operation and I'm facing *brain surgery*. Next month, Dr Drew wants to go ahead.'

I swallowed and looked down at my small arm. 'Can't you say you don't want to do it?'

Jack snorted and shook his head. 'It's not up to me, is it.' I didn't like Jack's glare. It was as if he hated the whole world, me included.

He lay down facing the window again. I stayed on his bed for a while, not saying anything.

Finally I went back to bed.

Everything was different after that.

Jack, Erin and I were still in the same room together, but we didn't connect the way we had at first. We kept to ourselves, doing our stuff without talking. It was as if an invisible barrier had come down between us.

After another round of tests in the morning, I sat in bed and played with my third arm, twirling the wrist and moving the fingers, marvelling that it had grown.

I stopped as soon as Mum walked in. It

wasn't so much the look on her face as *where* she looked. Her eyes slid to the side, away from my arm – away from *me*. It wasn't until I tucked my new arm neatly inside a sleeve that she looked at me and smiled. Even during tests that morning she'd kept her back turned, pretending to look out the window. I didn't need to ask what she had been thinking.

Not long now until this will all be over.
Not long until we can forget . . .

That night, a cry woke me from a light sleep. I slipped out of bed and padded across to Erin.

'Are you ok—' I began, then stopped when Erin murmured something and rolled over, her face twitching in a dream. She had cried out in her sleep.

I sighed and looked out the window. It was raining again. I looked back at a lump of a wing under the sheet. *Just two more days until her operation . . .*

There was no way I could go back to sleep. For something to do, I tiptoed over to Jack's bed and peered at him in the dim light.

'Don't think you can sneak up on me,' he mumbled, turning over and looking at me properly.

'If you could stop your operation, would you?' I asked, straight out.

Jack sat up and breathed in slowly. 'Yes,' he said clearly. 'I would.'

'What if it meant showing everyone . . . showing the whole world?'

One of Jack's eyebrows cocked. 'What are you up to?'

I shrugged. I hadn't really thought it through, but at the back of my mind, I did have an idea. Not a very good one, but it seemed better than nothing.

'Come on,' I said. 'Help me get into that office again.'

Once Jack had worked his magic with the keypad and we were inside, I sat in the swivel chair and turned the computer on.

Jack sat on the edge of the desk, swinging one leg. 'So . . . what? You're going to set up an online freak show?'

'If everyone knows what's going on, it won't be so easy for them to just . . .' I trailed off, watching the screen going through its start-up. 'Anyway, this thing is probably password protected.'

Miraculously it wasn't. Maybe Dr Drew figured two locked doors would be enough to keep people out.

'Freak show, here we come,' said Jack.

The next thing I knew, my new hand was resting on the mouse and the online world was at my fingertips. If I'd been unsure how I felt about my new arm, I wasn't wondering anymore. It felt so good to be doing things with it, to be *using* it, rather than holding it out to be poked and studied for the best way to have it removed.

It was easy to find some good photos saved in a file on the desktop – including a baby foot with seven toes and someone with a hand growing out of their shoulder. I cropped the photos carefully so that you couldn't see any faces then saved them as a series of stills in a movie file so that it would work on YouTube.

'You realise they'll just think it's a hoax,' said Jack over my shoulder. 'Half the stuff online is fake.'

'Yeah, but if I can get the news networks interested . . .' I searched for the contact details of all the major newspapers and TV stations around the country. Working fast, I typed a group email inviting them to come and interview us at the children's hospital and added a link to the photos.

'Do you think they'll come?' asked Jack when I'd finished.

'Probably not,' I said, but it still felt good to have done something.

On our way back to bed, our steps were lighter somehow.

The next morning, a hand shook my shoulder. I was awake in a flash.

'Come listen to this,' said Jack.

We snuck down the corridor and stopped behind a corner near the nurses' station.

Something was going on. Phones were ringing and people were talking over each other.

' . . . call security . . .'

'I don't know how it got out.'

'. . . we'll need someone to make a statement.'

I looked at Jack. 'Reporters?'

He nodded, grinning. 'They've been stopped at the ground floor.'

I peeked around the corner, not that I was worried we'd be caught. Everyone seemed too busy to care what we were doing.

'They won't let any reporters up here,' I said, stating the obvious.

For a while we were quiet, listening and watching, enjoying the fact that we'd caused a commotion.

'You know . . . there's nothing stopping *us* from getting down to *them*,' said Jack quietly. 'Nothing except a keypad or two.'

I looked at him. 'Are you sure?'

He nodded. 'Let's do it.'

11

Erin watched me pull on jeans and a T-shirt. I tried to act as though nothing was going on.

'Where are you going? Can I come too?' she asked, once I was dressed.

So much for my acting. I shook my head. 'Stay here, okay?'

'No!' She stamped a foot. 'Tell me!'

'Brooke, *come on*,' called Jack from the doorway.

I looked back at Erin and knelt so I was her height. 'We're going to sneak down and show media people what's . . . different about us. But you have to stay here.'

'No! I'm coming too.'

I shook my head as Erin put her hands on her hips. 'I want to show them my wings and you can't stop me.'

'Come on!' called Jack again.

84

I sighed. 'Okay.'

Holding Erin by the hand, we made our way down the corridor to the nurses' station. It was quiet by now. One nurse was on the phone but everyone else had disappeared. When she turned away to look at a computer screen we snuck past, making straight for the keypad beside the sliding doors.

Jack had them open before the nurse had any idea what was going on.

'Wait!' she called. 'What are you—'

But the doors had closed behind us.

An alarm whirred to life. It was so loud that it made my teeth ache. For a moment I was lost, disoriented.

'The lift . . . this way!' said Jack.

We started up the hall, holding Erin's hands between us, and then slowed when a woman in a guard uniform came round the corner. She saw us, and began to run.

Jack swore and I turned to see what he already had: two more guards coming from the other way. We were trapped.

'Quick,' I said, pulling Erin with one hand

and jabbing the other at the keypad. 'Get us back in!'

'What?' Jack had no idea what I was thinking, but he did as I asked. The guards, too, pulled up and slowed as they watched us break back into Ward 5G.

Inside, the nurse had her back to us, phone to her ear.

I dashed up the hall, tugging Erin behind me. She opened her wings so that she half-ran half-glided to keep up.

Jack was still holding her other hand. 'What are you doing?' he yelled, panting. 'That's a dead end.'

Sure, it was a dead end in the real world but it was also a gateway to the CCTV network of the entire hospital.

Working fast, I brought up the closed circuit network of surveillance cameras for Ward 5G. I was glad to have my extra arm to speed things up. There were even more cameras than I'd realised. I found the camera at the nurses' station and brought up that view.

'Hey!' cried Erin. 'I know them.'

I couldn't help a chuckle. The view showed the guards and nurse all huddled around a monitor. They were doing the same as us, looking through the CCTV network. For a while, we looked at them looking for us.

They had a problem, though. The office we were in didn't have any cameras, so they had no idea where we were. They kept pointing at the screen and scratching their heads. After a while they began to search through the ward, looking in cupboards and under beds.

We didn't have much time. In a new window I brought up a map of the hospital and worked out the nearest exit from the doorway to our ward – not a lift, but a stairwell.

'Here,' I said, pointing. 'We have to get out of the ward again and bolt for the stairs.'

'That's a great idea,' said Jack dryly. 'But we have to *get out* again first . . .' He pointed at a view of the nurses' station. Two of the guards were still looking for us, but one was standing next to the exit.

Rats.

'What now, Brooke?' asked Erin. 'What are we going to do?' Her eyes were eager and trusting.

'We need a decoy,' Jack said, looking at Erin.

I crouched down to Erin's level, two hands on her shoulders and my third brushing a bit of hair behind her ear. 'Erin,' I said. 'We need the guards to chase you. If you can get them to do that then Jack and I can make it to the exit.'

'Why me?' she pouted.

'Because we'll be faster without you,' Jack said.

'Even *with* your wings,' I added, but I didn't tell her what I was really thinking: *this way I know you'll be safe.* 'Once everyone knows about us, they won't be able to hide you away. We'll make sure you get to show them your wings.'

'Promise?'

I didn't want to say it, but Erin's eyes gave me no choice. 'Okay, I promise.'

12

It wasn't easy watching Erin trot away. On the monitor, she looked so tiny.

Jack and I stayed in the office, watching her pass through each camera view as she ran the back way around to the other end of the hall leading to the exit doors. Just as we'd planned, the guard at the exit was the first to see her. He called out, and Erin turned and bolted.

I held my breath as the guard called out again. He looked up and down the hall, waiting for the others. Then he gave up and ran after Erin.

'Good man,' said Jack to the monitor.

Outside our door came the clatter of running feet, growing louder then fading as they passed.

Now was our time. Together we slipped out of the office and bolted straight to the sliding doors. I could hear shouting from the direction Erin had run but I couldn't see what was happening.

We dashed through the doors and into the hall. This time the alarm didn't even sound.

Without a word we raced for the stairwell, pausing only to make sure the door didn't slam behind us. Jack was ahead of me, taking two stairs at a time. The first landing had a small window and a camera mounted in the corner of the ceiling. I turned my face away from it. Would anyone still be watching the CCTV?

When I made it to the ground floor, Jack placed his hand on the doorknob. 'Ready?' he asked.

'I ... I guess,' I stammered, but suddenly I wasn't sure. Now that we were so close to showing ourselves, I couldn't help thinking about Mum: *I can't stand to think how they'd treat her. The awful things they'd say.*

What would she say once she realised I'd shown the whole world?

'We don't have to ...' Jack began.

Then, from outside at street level, came a scream followed by cries of alarm. We were at the window just in time to see something glide past. Bigger than a bird, with wings held wide.

It was Erin.

'Oh . . . man!' cried Jack, nudging me out of the way and straining to see out the window.

At the door I squashed an ear to the crack, trying to hear what was going on. I couldn't hear a thing.

'Now?' I asked Jack. When he nodded, I pushed the door open.

Walking through the entrance to the foyer was Erin. Her wings were folded shut. Behind her trailed a bunch of reporters, camera lenses pointed at her.

It was almost eerie. They were all quiet . . . stunned by what they had seen, I guess. It was as if they were too shocked even to mob her. They just followed to see what she would do next.

Together we ran for Erin. I picked her up in a hug. 'Erin? Are you okay?'

She smiled. 'Those guards were about to catch me but I didn't let them. I ran out onto the balcony and I did it, Brooke. I flew!'

I couldn't help laughing. I'd been worried about keeping her safe, and she was braver than I had been. 'Yes, Erin,' I smiled. 'You did it.'

Jack was beaming when I looked his way. 'Come on, you two.'

Together we turned to face the reporters. To one side I could see Dr Drew walking towards us with a phone to his ear.

I looked at Jack.

He nodded at me and winked, so I clenched my fists – all three of them – and raised my right arms in the air. *Look at this.*

For a moment, the room stayed quiet. A camera flashed. Then another. And another. Suddenly, all was movement around us. Two reporters pushed closer. More seemed to come from nowhere.

'What's your name?'

'Did you send the email?'

Microphones and other gadgets were shoved in our faces. Jack crouched, said something to Erin, then lifted her onto his shoulders. I was glad she wasn't being smothered. A woman in a white coat asked the reporters to stand back before saying something to Jack. I didn't hear what she said but then Jack nodded and pointed to the back of his head. The woman rubbed her chin, nodding. I wanted to ask who she was – some kind of scientist maybe – but a familiar voice to one side made me turn.

'Brooke!' Mum stood between two reporters, her mouth open and her forehead crinkled in confusion. She rushed forward as if ready to spring into action, to hide me away. As she came close, though, she must have realised that she couldn't hide me now. She stopped and shook her head helplessly.

'Mum . . .' I stepped towards her, holding my arms out, palms up. For a moment, I wasn't sure what to say. 'I'm sorry . . . I don't—' I shook my head. 'It . . . it's *my arm*.' Flashes were still going off around us, but I barely noticed. All that mattered was Mum.

For a while she stared at me. Her eyes slid down to my new arm. They lingered as if looking at it for the first time. Then she stepped closer and took my new hand in hers, cupping it gently and stroking my small wrist with the backs of her fingers.

The feel of her touch ran up my arm and into my chest. It made me breathe in, tears in my eyes. This was the first time anyone had touched my arm like that.

Like she was touching *me*.

After a while Mum looked up and smiled, tears in her eyes too. 'It reminds me of when you were a baby,' she whispered.

I threw my arms around her and squeezed. More flashes went off.

When I pulled back to glance over at the others, Jack was still talking to the woman in the white coat. Erin grinned and waved at me from his shoulders.

When I turned back to Mum she shook her head but still managed a smile. 'I hope you're sure about this, Brooke.'

I nodded. *Yes, I'm sure.* More than anything I felt an enormous sense of relief. I wasn't sure what to expect from here, but I was glad I didn't have to hide my arm anymore.

As I waved back at Erin I felt something on the back of my left arm, halfway between my elbow and my shoulder.

The fingers of my right hand hovered over the spot . . .

IT BEGAN WITH A TINGLE

Omigosh! I knew that sensation; I'd felt it before.

It wasn't sore or itchy the way a bite might feel.

It was tingling and weirdly warm . . .

1

LET ME MAKE ONE THING CLEAR: I didn't steal anything from the Big Cow Cafe. Why would I? I don't even *like* smoked-trout sandwiches, and I'd already had lunch – a steaming sausage roll with zigzag sauce.

I was only in the cafe because my older brother, Connor, was selling bait worms to the cafe owner. That guy sure used a lot of fish in his cafe.

The cafe owner paid Connor while I waited beside the sandwich counter, staring up at the ceiling fans and sniffing the air – fresh cakes, warm pies, even the coffee smelled good.

But as we headed for the door, the owner rushed around the counter yelling, 'Stop! Stop, thief!'

I glanced around, looking for the thief.

The owner raced up to me, his fat cheeks wobbling. He grabbed something poking out of the top of my gym bag. It was a smoked-trout sandwich.

'Why didn't you pay for this?' he asked gruffly. His breath smelled like stale coffee.

My neck burned and I barely managed to shake my head. I hadn't taken the sandwich. How did it end up in my bag?

'Jamie!' hissed Connor behind me.

A lady with sunglasses whispered to her granddaughter and pointed at me.

'How old are you, young man?' asked the cafe owner and crossed his arms.

'Eleven,' I squeaked, looking around at all the faces. 'But I didn't take the sandwich. I promise! How could I have reached it?'

Everyone watched as I walked back to the counter and tried to reach over. There was no way! Somehow, I would have had to extend my arm over the counter and then back under the glass covering, like an elephant's trunk curling under to reach its mouth. Even on tiptoes my hand barely made it to the other side.

'See?' I said, jerking a hand into thin air.

Everyone turned to the cafe owner. 'But how did the sandwich get in your bag?' he asked.

Everyone turned back to me. 'I . . .' My shoulders slumped. 'I don't know.' My face burned mega-atomic-red.

'I'm not going to call the police,' said the cafe owner. 'But I would like to speak to your parents.'

'Mum's at the supermarket,' said Connor helpfully.

Thanks, Connor.

It was so embarrassing. The owner made me sit out the back, scowling at the stupid sandwich on the bench beside me, waiting for Connor and Mum.

After a while, my face stopped burning quite so hot, and something began to nag at my mind.

Even though I hadn't taken the sandwich, I had the uneasy feeling that this was a weird kind of punishment I deserved. Maybe it was happening because of what I'd done two weeks earlier – something so bad that I still felt sick just thinking about it.

When Mum turned up with Connor, her face was bright red too. She glanced at me, then started babbling to the owner and pushing a ten-dollar note into his hands.

My heart sank. *Thanks a lot, Mum. Thanks for sticking up for me*. She just assumed I'd done it, without even asking me.

Then I realised what was happening. Mum knew what I'd done two weeks earlier. So why should she be on my side now? I wasn't her 'good little Jamie' anymore. Since that day two weeks ago, everything had been different.

In fact, stealing a sandwich was nothing compared to what I had done.

At one point, Mum leaned in to the owner and whispered, 'We have some issues going on at home.'

I closed my eyes and wished I could disappear. *Please don't tell him what I did. Please don't tell him . . .*

When I opened my eyes, they were both looking at me. The owner had his head tilted to the side, as if he felt sorry for me.

I gulped and tried to stop looking guilty.

'Never again, okay?' said the cafe owner, and wiggled a fat finger from side to side.

I tried one last time. 'I didn't . . .' I stopped and sighed. What was the point? I looked down and nodded.

As we walked home, Connor hung back so that Mum and I could walk together, but I knew that he would stick close enough to hear what we were saying.

Mum tried to rest her hand on the back of my neck as we walked, but I shrugged her off. I was angry that Mum thought I had stolen the sandwich. I was angry and scared. I wasn't used to this kind of thing happening to me. Connor was the one who always got into trouble.

At first we said nothing, but Mum kept fiddling with her earring, so I knew she was working up to saying something.

I knew what it would be, too. It would be about Monty.

'I just don't understand,' Mum said eventually.

'No, it doesn't make sense, does it?' I said hopefully, stepping over a puddle on the footpath.

'You've never stolen anything in your life!' Mum said.

'So why would I start now?' I said, but my voice sounded thin. 'Think about it, Mum. I didn't steal the sandwich. I promise!'

Mum shook her head sadly. 'But how did it get into your bag? I mean, no one else could have put it there.'

'Yeah? Well it wasn't ME,' I yelled. I had no idea who had swiped the sandwich, but I couldn't shake the feeling that I was being punished.

Two weeks ago, Monty died. And it was all my fault.

2

On the day Monty died, I was home on my own, which didn't happen very often. I had a long list of things to do – handstands in the hall, computer games in Connor's room – but first I was going to sneak some ice-cream.

After I waved goodbye to the car, I headed straight to the freezer, grabbing a spoon on my way. Who needs a bowl when you're home alone? Yum.

That's when I heard a knock at the door.

It doesn't take long for your life to change forever.

I will always remember exactly what the man said when I opened the door: 'Do you own a scraggy black dog? I'm so sorry. We've run over someone's dog.'

For some reason, the way he called Monty a 'scraggy black dog' made the whole thing even worse. I loved Monty just the way he was; I loved his curly hair. He had been the family dog, but he had played with me most of all.

At first I was in a daze. As the man carried Monty into our front garden I stayed quiet. It wasn't until after the man had gone that I realised how it had happened. In my rush to get back inside for ice-cream and computer games, I had forgotten to shut the gate. It was my fault that Monty had run onto the road.

I knelt next to Monty feeling dizzy with guilt. He just lay there, still and floppy. I wanted to shake him, to try to wake him up, but I knew he was dead. Blades of grass rested against his nose, but he didn't sneeze or move his head.

I loved Monty so much. If only I had shut the gate, then he'd still be alive.

It seemed like hours that I knelt beside him in the garden, sniffling and waiting for my family to come home. But it was even worse when they did.

As they climbed out of the car I started crying, hard and loud. But the words still came out, the words that were spinning around my head: 'I left the gate open.'

Mum hugged me while Dad and Connor leaned over Monty. After a while, Dad went to dig a grave in the backyard.

I gave Monty one last pat and unbuckled his collar. When Dad came back pushing the wheel-barrow, I turned away. I couldn't watch.

Monty's favourite stick was lying on the grass.

I picked it up too. The wood was smooth because all the bark had been chewed off. Monty loved playing fetch with that old stick. For the rest of the afternoon I held that stick and the collar to my chest.

None of my family yelled at me or even seemed annoyed. They just looked at me sadly; even Connor said nothing about what I had done.

And that made me feel even worse. I had done something awful, and I deserved to be punished for it – grounded for a year or forced to quit gymnastics. But no one said anything at all.

From then on, the guilt sat inside me like a disease. I could feel it living in me, making my breath smell bad. I could see it in their faces when my family looked at me.

It changed the way I felt inside.

Now, as we walked home from the Big Cow Cafe, Mum asked a heap of questions about my friends and whether I had told them about Monty. 'What about your friends at gymnastics?'

She seemed to have decided that I had stolen the sandwich because of Monty, as though I had turned to the dark side now. Kill your dog, become a thief – it was all a natural course of events.

But I just felt sick. I couldn't talk to Mum about any of it. I couldn't bear to keep thinking about it.

When we got home, Dad looked up from the newspaper. 'Is everything okay?' he said as I passed.

But I just kept going straight to my room and slammed the door.

I lay on my bed and buried my face in my quilt, crying until the light blue cover had a dark blue patch around my face. There were a lot of tear-stained patches on my quilt.

Eventually the tears slowed. I sat on the edge of my bed and reached into my gym bag for a drink of water. But as I pulled it out, I gasped and hugged the bottle to my chest.

There, in my gym bag, was the trout sandwich. The one I'd been accused of stealing. But it wasn't sitting quietly as it had been in the shop.

It was jumping up and down.

3

I stared at the trout sandwich, too amazed to move. It was flopping around like a fish out of water.

With one massive leap, the sandwich was out of the bag and onto my bed. It started flopping towards me.

Eek! I pushed myself backwards off my bed, hitting the bookcase with a thud and dropping my bottle on the floor. Water trickled out of the bottle and onto the carpet, but I wasn't worried about that.

The sandwich looked like a freaky ocean beast. Cling wrap flopped around it like a limp fin and lettuce trailed after it like seaweed.

The sandwich flopped onto the floor and jumped towards the bottle I'd dropped. It landed in the wet patch on my carpet and lay there flapping, like a kid splashing in water.

I stared at it with my mouth open. It was the most amazing thing I had ever seen. Was the sandwich somehow alive?

I found a ruler on my bookcase and knelt on the floor. Using one end of the ruler I dragged open the last bit of cling wrap. Then I flipped the top piece of bread over as if I was flipping a pancake. Underneath were slices of tomato, some floppy lettuce . . . and six or seven slivers of shiny trout.

For a moment, nothing moved. Then a single piece of trout started jumping. Flip, flop . . . flip flop . . .

It looked exactly like a fish trying to flip itself back into the water. Except, it was just a *piece* of fish. A freaky fishy blob.

The trout flicked what looked like its tail-end, flopped itself into the mouth of the bottle opening, slithered down the neck, and was soon swishing around in the water left inside.

The next thing I knew, the other pieces of fish were flipping across my bedroom floor. They looked as if they were having a party, dancing to music that I couldn't hear.

One by one, they dived into the bottle. The last piece was wider than the others, and wider than the mouth of the bottle. It sat for a while on the carpet. Then it rolled itself into a tube and wiggled into the bottle opening.

I shook my head in amazement. Somehow, those pieces of fish were still alive, and had been searching for water all along. They must have jumped the sandwich into my gym bag.

I lay on my stomach and peered into the bottle. I couldn't take my eyes off those fish (well, those fish *pieces*, I guess). They were supremely brilliant. It was as though the universe was giving me a second chance, a way to make up for what I had done to Monty. Here was something amazing and alive that needed my help. If I could help these pieces of trout and keep them safe – then maybe I could forgive myself for Monty.

Water was the first thing my fish needed. A bucketful. The bottle was way too small for them.

I snuck into the laundry and filled an old green bucket with the tap on a quiet trickle. I didn't want anyone to hear me and start asking difficult questions.

The bucket was heavier than I expected and it bumped against the edge of the laundry trough as I lifted it out, sloshing cold water onto my legs and shoes. But I didn't mind. It felt good having something important to do.

I opened the laundry door and listened.

Everything was quiet. I could faintly hear my parents talking in the kitchen.

Struggling with the bucket, I started down the hall, but just as I passed Connor's bedroom, the door opened.

Typical. I stopped, unsure what to do.

Connor leaned against the doorframe, grinning. 'So what's the real story with the sandwich?' he whispered. Then he looked at the bucket of water and my wet shoes. 'This one's going to be good.' He stood back so that I could walk into his room.

I glanced across at my own room, wishing I could get back there without Connor trying to follow.

'Come on, Jamie,' Connor said impatiently. 'I won't tell.'

I knew he wouldn't tell, but I still wasn't sure what to say. I set the bucket on the floor of his room and rubbed the palm of my hand where the handle had been digging in.

Connor shut the door. 'So, spill the beans,' he said. 'Why did you steal the sandwich?' He leaned against the edge of his desk.

I looked down at the bucket. 'It's these amazing fish, see,' I sighed. The truth sounded so weird . . .

Connor frowned at the bucket. 'It's not for some boring school project, is it?'

I rolled my eyes. 'Oh, shut up, Connor.' He always teased me for trying at school. Even if I was just reading a book, Connor always said something smart about it. So I looked him straight in the eye, and lied.

'I was going to hide the fish sandwich in Mr Murray's desk so that it stank the whole place out.'

There was a long pause as Connor looked at me – curious and impressed. He'd never looked at me that way before.

I held his gaze, almost smiling. It made me feel strong and powerful, as if I was a dark, mysterious criminal. *(See that scar on my finger? It's from wrestling a thrashing killer trout. And see that wild look in my eye? It's from seeing things that you would never believe.)*

After a while, he cracked up laughing. 'Not bad, not bad . . . I'm impressed.'

Then I thought of something. 'Actually, I was wondering, when you sell worms up at the cafe, have you ever noticed anything . . . *strange* about the fish that get caught?'

Connor frowned. 'Strange in what way?'

'Nothing. I was just wondering.'

'That guy buys heaps of worms, though. I think the fish keep stealing them from the hook.' He shrugged. 'Lucky there are so many in our backyard. You can help me dig for worms next time if you want,' he said.

'Thanks,' I said, and picked up the bucket.

Somehow, it didn't seem quite so heavy anymore.

Back in my own room, I put the bucket on the carpet and rubbed my aching hands again. The fish pieces were still flapping in the bottom of the bottle, right where I had left them.

Gently, I lifted the bottle just above the bucket's waterline, and tipped. Water trickled from the bottle, but nothing else did. The fish didn't fall out.

'Come on.' I jiggled my bottle, trying to shake out the fish. Nothing moved.

I jiggled again, a bit rougher this time. With a series of sliding plops, all seven pieces slipped into the bucket and began sinking. When they were about halfway down, they shook their tail ends and began to swim. Pretty amazing.

Slowly the fish pieces swam faster and faster until they were bumping up against each other. There was so much action in the bucket that water splashed over the edge. It was hard to see what was going on. A couple of pieces jumped up and landed back in the water.

At one point the whole bucket rocked. I held onto the rim in case it tipped over. Water frothed and bubbled and spilled onto the carpet. My hands were soaking wet.

Suddenly the splashing stopped.

Biting my lip, I peered inside. A single piece of trout floated in the water. It curved itself around one side of the bucket in a crescent shape. It swished its tail end peacefully.

'Oh . . . wow!' I could hardly believe it. This fish was magic. It had to be. Somehow it was able to *heal* itself . . . it was trying to become whole again.

I leaned back against my bed with the bucket in front of me and shook my wet hands. I could see a photo of Monty on my desk. I'd left his favourite stick next to it and hung his collar on a post of my bed. In the photo, Monty was sitting with his ears pricked up. He looked really smart. Not *scraggy* at all.

'What do you think, Monty?' I asked.

I was getting a bit teary, so I peered back in the bucket. I didn't know how it had managed to reform. But I did know one thing – this fish wanted to live.

All through dinner I stayed quiet, wondering about the trout. Would it grow eyes and a mouth? Would it need food?

Whatever happened, I would look after it. Then, once it was fully re-formed, I would take it to a river and let it go. It would have a new life, swimming free.

That night I went to bed feeling better than I had in two weeks. I snuggled under the covers, listening to the faint swishing of water in the dark.

Maybe I had messed up with Monty and let him get killed, but here was my second chance. I would do anything to help the trout live.

6

The next morning I woke up early and checked the fish. Had it survived the night? Was it still alright?

But I didn't need to worry. My trout was more than alright. It was awesome.

In the bucket was a normal, everyday trout. It had eyes, a mouth and a tail. A pretty pinky-orange stripe extended down its side. Its scales shimmered in the water.

'Hello,' I said. I wasn't surprised to see that the fish had re-formed. Not after everything else that had happened. But I was a little disappointed. Now I had to set it free in the river. It was the only right thing to do.

'Worms,' I said to myself. I'd feed it some worms. Then I'd take it to the river in the afternoon.

I was pulling on my shorts when the trout jumped into the air. With a flick of its tail it sprinkled water in an arc across the carpet. A few drops made it as far as my desk. The fish landed safely back in the bucket.

I sat on my bed and hugged my knees. What would happen next?

But the fish just swished in the bucket.

Oh well. That was still a clever thing to do. And it gave me an idea. 'Splash! That's what I'll call you!' A pet needs a name. I scratched my head. 'But are you a boy or a girl fish?'

Splash kept swishing.

I shrugged again. 'Let's just say you're a girl for now.' Maybe it was because Monty had been a boy – I don't know – but I liked the idea of Splash being a girl.

She must have been happy too because she did a single jump in the air. With a clever flick of her tail, Splash sprinkled water over the top of my desk.

Monty's photo! I didn't want that getting wet. I went to move the photo out of the splash zone but my hand froze in midair.

Beside the photo, and wet from Splash's tricks, lay Monty's favourite stick. Wherever a drop of water had landed, tiny leaves had sprouted. Down one end there were even a few tiny roots.

'Wow!' I said. 'How did you do that?'

Splash jumped proudly and landed back in the bucket.

I picked up the stick and peered at it. Tiny, bright-green leaves had formed on the ends of the twigs.

This was amazing! Splash didn't just know how to re-form herself; she could bring other things back to life. I'd pulled the stick off an apple tree at my cousin's farm last year. It had been chewed and chucked around ever since then.

Now here it was in my hands, alive again.

Splash turned in the bucket and jumped like a dolphin, trying to see out, I guessed.

When she saw Monty's old collar hooked on the end of my bed, she stopped jumping and swished in the water again. It looked as if she was working up to something.

With another jump and a clever flick of her tail, Splash sprinkled water over the collar.

I watched with one hand over my mouth, almost too amazed to breathe.

For a moment, I thought the collar had disappeared. I peered close, trying to see what was going on.

The collar *had* disappeared. At the end of my bed stood something dark-brown and tiny. It looked up at me and said, 'Mooooer.'

7

'A cow!' I yelled. 'A cow!'

A teensy weensy tiny little cow stood in front of me! I wanted to kiss the fish and hug the cow. It was all so amazing. Splash was bringing life to things that were already dead!

She jumped proudly and landed back in the bucket.

I knelt beside my bed and peered at the cow. 'You're so small!' I whispered. It sniffed the quilt and tried to nibble. Then it looked up at me and blinked.

When I turned to Splash, she was low in the

water, curled around the side of the bucket. She looked as if she was resting.

The cow was wandering around my bed. I didn't want it to fall off, so I arranged some pillows along the edge. Then I found my old farm set at the back of my wardrobe and set up the fence under my bed. If Connor came snooping in here, or worse, Mum . . .

As I worked, I thought about the things that Splash had done. New leaves and roots on an apple-tree branch were amazing. But a real live cow? Monty's collar had turned into a cow.

I leaned back on my heels, thinking and watching the cow.

The collar had been made of leather, and leather came from cows . . . It wasn't just *any* cow in front of me, it must have been the same cow that had been used to make Monty's collar. The same, except smaller.

Years ago, a normal-sized version of that cow had been wandering through a paddock, just like this tiny one in front of me.

It was a strange feeling.

I didn't feel sad about the cow, or angry at the people who had killed it. But I did feel weird, as we had been connected to the cow all this time and didn't know it – like a neighbour who you live next to for years and never find out their name.

I herded the cow into a box with my hand, and released it under my bed. Then I found a plastic lid and filled it with water from the bathroom for the cow to drink. Perfect.

Now that the cow was safe, I looked around my room as though seeing it with new eyes. What other things could Splash bring back to life? I had feathers in my quilt, sheepskin boots – there were so many things. But I didn't have time for that yet.

Splash needed worms. The stick needed soil. And the cow needed grass. I had jobs to do.

Morning sun was shining through the window in the kitchen when I walked in.

'Jamie?' Mum looked up from beside the coffee maker.

Connor was standing at the bench, yawning and pouring rice bubbles into a bowl.

'Morning!' I called, and kept going. There wasn't much point talking to Mum these days. I was tired of her watching me with worried eyes.

In the backyard I found the ice-cream container Connor used to collect worms and filled it with fresh soil. Through the kitchen window, I could see Mum watching me work. I ignored her as I pulled up a clump of grass for the cow and dug up worms for Splash, placing them on top of the soil.

Instead of going back into the kitchen I headed inside through the laundry.

The door had just slammed behind me when Mum appeared. She was playing madly with her earring again.

'Jamie, what were you doing out in the garden?' she asked, frowning at my ice-cream container.

I looked down at the worms curling up on the soil. 'Just . . . something for a school project.' I didn't like lying, but there was no way I was going to tell her about Splash.

'Digging up worms?' asked Mum, peering into my bowl. She leaned close, trying to look me in the eye. 'Exactly what is this project about?'

'Why do I have to tell you?' I snapped. 'Why can't you just *trust me* for once?'

Mum's whole face flushed. 'Jamie, I don't think you've been telling the truth,' she said. 'I want you to tell me what's going on.'

We stood in the laundry – me and Mum – glaring at each other. She put her hands on her hips; I shifted my feet, trying to think what to say. I just wanted everyone to leave me alone to look after Splash.

'There's nothing to worry about, Mum,' I said softly.

'That's just it,' Mum said. 'I *am* worried. You've been acting so strangely.'

I didn't know what else to say, but Connor did. He stood in the doorway behind me. 'Listen, Mum,' he said. 'It's just a dumb school project, nothing to worry about.' The faintest smile flickered on his lips. 'Jamie told me all about it,' he said. 'They're doing fish projects in science. That's all that was going on yesterday too. It's really boring.'

Connor was good at this!

Mum was fiddling with her earring again. 'But why the secret? Why *steal* the sandwich?' she said.

'I needed the trout in the sandwich for the project,' I said quickly. 'I just kept it all secret because I didn't want anyone to copy.'

Connor glanced at me and smiled. 'Jamie the square,' he said. 'That's our Jamie!'

We were doing a great job; at least I thought so. But Mum wasn't convinced.

'So you admit you took the sandwich?' she said slowly. Then she held out her hands and shook her head. 'But you told me you didn't! And it's not *like you*, Jamie.'

Mum was right. It *wasn't* like me to steal and lie. Yesterday I would have been glad to hear her say that. But it didn't make me glad now; it made me angry. I took a step towards her.

'I wouldn't steal a sandwich?' I said. 'That's a bit late, Mum.' My voice was loud, but I didn't care. 'Why didn't you say that in the cafe yesterday? Why didn't you stick up for me?'

Mum stopped fiddling with her earring and

looked at Connor. He was quiet too, for once.

They both stared at me. I didn't get angry very often. But I didn't let up. I wanted to make Mum feel bad.

'Why didn't you stick up for me, Mum? And why are you so worried now?'

For a while we were quiet, but I could feel the answer hovering in the air around us. I imagined them thinking it, but not being able to say it.

It was Monty. That was why Mum hadn't stuck up for me in the Big Cow Cafe. And that was why she was so worried now.

I wanted to keep yelling, to force Mum to say it: *Since you let Monty get killed, I don't know if I can trust you anymore.*

But Mum didn't say it. 'I don't know, Jamie,' she said quietly. She let her hand drop. 'I just don't know anymore.'

You mean you don't know ME anymore, I wanted to say. But I pushed past them both and walked straight to my room.

I just wanted to lie on my bed and feel sad about Monty. And angry at Mum. But I had to check Splash first, and the cow.

I pulled the bucket from under my desk and sighed. Splash jiggled her tail. She snapped at the worms happily.

I was just about to check the cow when Connor poked his head into my room. 'Can I come in?'

'Just shut the door, okay?' I said. I didn't bother to hide Splash.

Connor shut the door. Then he slapped his hand over his mouth. 'Geez, how come you have a fish?' He shot me that curious, impressed look again. 'Where did you get it from?'

Splash swished in the bucket at our feet.

'Um, the cafe . . .' I looked sideways at Connor.

But he didn't seem worried about Splash. He was frowning and clutching his hands together. 'Jamie, are you okay?' he asked seriously.

I nodded. 'Thanks for helping me with Mum,' I said. 'She's really crazy at the moment.'

'She's worried about you, Jamie,' Connor said, and shuffled his feet.

I wondered if I should show Connor what Splash could do. The apple-tree stick was still lying on my desk, complete with its tiny leaves.

'Do you miss Monty?' Connor said, looking down.

I frowned and swallowed. This was the first time Connor had mentioned Monty since he died. It felt good to hear his name. But the question surprised me. I wasn't *allowed* to miss Monty. It was my fault he was dead. When I thought of Monty now, all I could feel was pain and regret. I wasn't allowed to miss him.

I stared down at Splash. 'I feel so bad for what I did,' I said. 'I wish I could . . . you know . . . fix it. Make it alright again. But there's nothing I can do.'

'Jamie, you don't have to—' Connor started to say.

But something I had just said echoed in my mind. *How can I fix what I did? How can I . . .*

'Oh WOW!' I yelled. 'THAT'S IT!'

I was delighted and terrified all at once. Why hadn't I thought of it straight away?

I grabbed Connor's arm.

'Monty! Monty!' I cried. 'I know how to fix Monty!'

I jumped up and down, yelling and laughing about Monty. Of course! Splash had brought the cow and the stick back to life. Why couldn't she bring Monty back to life too?

Connor was watching me carefully, as if he thought I was mad.

Fair enough. He could think I was mad for now. But I was too excited to explain.

'Come and watch this!' I said to Connor. This was going to be brilliant! I was so glad that Splash had jumped into my bag. It was so worth being called a thief.

I grabbed her bucket and headed the back way out to Monty's grave in the backyard. Connor followed.

I put the bucket down on the grass near the grave and stood back. I imagined Monty lying down there. Waiting.

'Okay, Splash, do your stuff!' I said happily. But then I thought of something. We didn't want Monty coming back to life while he was buried under all that dirt. 'Wait! We need a spade,' I said to Connor. My heart was pounding.

Connor's face went white. His mouth dropped open.

'It's okay, Connor,' I said. 'Just wait until you see.'

But he turned and ran inside.

I grabbed the spade from where I had been digging up worms. I knew it seemed crazy to be digging up a pet dog that had been dead for two weeks, but everyone would understand once Monty came back to life.

Digging was harder than I expected. Even though the ground had been softened by rain, I had to jump up and down on the spade to force it into the dirt.

I had only managed one spadeful when Connor came back with Mum and Dad.

'Jamie, what are you doing?' Dad's voice was quiet.

I stopped digging. 'It's okay, Dad,' I said. 'Just trust me with this.'

Mum had her hands over her mouth. She looked as if she wanted to cry.

'Put the spade down, Jamie,' Dad said. 'We need to talk.'

'No, Dad! I have to do this.' I jumped on the spade to dig it into the ground. Then I levered the handle down to push up the dirt.

Dad put his hands on the spade.

'No!' I yelled.

Slowly and forcefully, Dad pulled the spade out of my hands.

'Okay, I know this seems crazy,' I said. 'But this trout is magic. She can bring Monty back to life.'

'Where did you get that fish?' Dad said carefully, pointing at Splash.

'It's a trout!' I yelled. 'It's from the Big Cow Cafe. It's the one from the sandwich.' It sounded crazy, even to me.

Dad watched me with wide eyes. Mum had her hands over her face, sobbing. Even Connor looked scared.

'Alright, follow me,' I said. I picked up Splash in her bucket and headed back to my room. I just had to show them the cow. Maybe I could get Splash to do some more magic and turn a feather into a duck. Once my family saw that, they would all *help* me dig up Monty.

We all crowded into my room. No more secrets. No more hiding. Everything was going to be alright.

But as I put down Splash's bucket, I let out a gasp. Everything was *not* alright.

Lying in the shadow of my bed was Monty's old collar. No cow. Just a lifeless piece of leather.

I pulled out the collar and stared at it in my hands. What did this mean?

'This can't be happening!' I cried. It had all been so perfect. Splash was the only one who could help Monty come back to life. I helped Splash, and Splash would help Monty. It all made sense.

'Splash?' I said, gripping the rim of the bucket.

I gasped again. She was curled around the side of the bucket, resting on the bottom. Some of her scales had fallen off and her pinky-orange skin looked blotchy and raw.

She didn't even move. Was something wrong with her? Did she need to go back to the river?

'What's going on, Jamie?' Mum asked. She looked down at Splash with her nose scrunched up.

But I wasn't giving up yet.

I stood up and grabbed the apple stick on my desk. Luckily, it was still covered in leaves. 'There!' I said, holding out the stick. 'See? It's Monty's old stick. Splash brought it back to life!'

Mum and Dad muttered something to each other, but Connor tilted his head.

I held it out in two hands, but Connor shrugged. 'It just looks like you broke it off a tree this morning.'

'Jamie, you have to let us help you,' Dad said.

'Just let me dig up Monty,' I pleaded. 'Please. It doesn't hurt anyone. Just let me try.'

But from the looks on my parents' faces, I realised that they would send me to the loony bin before they let me dig up Monty.

I felt like screaming. Nothing made sense anymore. The pieces of trout, the branch, the tiny cow . . . it had been *magic* . . .

But not magic enough.

Mum stepped forward and tried to hold my hands. 'Jamie, this business with Monty . . . It's making you sick.'

I shook my head.

'We're going to call a doctor who can help you.'

'A doctor?' I said quietly. I didn't need a doctor. I needed . . .

'I *killed* Monty,' I said slowly.

'Sweetheart.' Mum tried to hug me, but I was clear now.

I stood in front of my parents with my back straight, and looked them in the eye. I felt calm.

The time had come. Ever since I had left the gate open, I had been moving towards this moment.

'I killed Monty,' I said. 'Why aren't you mad at me? Why haven't you yelled at me?'

Mum and Dad just stared.

I said it again, slowly, so they'd have to respond: 'I. Killed. Monty.'

'It was an accident, sweetheart,' Mum said.

'What do you want us to do?' Dad asked and held his hands out helplessly.

'You're my parents! Yell at me! Make me pay for what I did.'

'You want us to punish you?' said Dad.

I deserved to be punished. I had to make up for what I had done to Monty. If Splash wasn't going to bring Monty back to life, I had to find another way to pay for what I did.

'Okay, we'll think of something,' Dad said. Mum patted my shoulder and they both left the room.

I sat on my bed with Connor.

'Do you believe me about the trout?' I asked.

Connor shrugged. 'I suppose so,' he said.

'You don't usually make up crazy things.' But he didn't look so sure of himself.

I started talking then. I told Connor everything – about the jumping sandwich and the pieces of trout. I told him about Splash doing magic on the apple stick and Monty's old collar. Through it all, he listened quietly. He didn't laugh or even shake his head.

At the end, all he said was, 'Jamie, you didn't kill Monty.'

'Yes I did.' I knew exactly what I had done. I would have to live with it for the rest of my life.

'You didn't kill Monty,' Connor said again. 'You left the gate open and Monty ran onto the road.'

I shrugged. 'It's the same thing.'

'No it's not,' Connor said. He spoke slowly, as though he was saying something very important. 'You made a mistake, but you didn't kill Monty.'

I sighed. 'It was my fault, Connor.'

Connor didn't say anything to that. He put his arm around my shoulders and gave me a squeeze.

We sat there, waiting for Mum and Dad to come back with my punishment. And I didn't even feel silly getting a hug from my brother.

11

The punishment my parents thought up was typical of them. At first it sounded silly, but after a while it made sense.

Remember Monty.

That was it – they wanted me to learn how to feel happy about Monty's life. No more feeling sad and guilty when I thought of him. I had to forgive myself for leaving the gate open, and I had to honour Monty's life.

All afternoon, we pulled out photos of Monty and talked about the funny things he used to do, like climb up the woodpile and through the shed window during a thunderstorm. Or the way he could snap up a piece of cheese that we rested on the tip of his nose.

It felt good to be with my family again. No more silent looks or worried sighs. I didn't have to feel scared about what they were thinking or worry that they hated me for what I had done.

And I realised that I wanted to say sorry. Not just to Monty, but to Mum and Dad and Connor. Monty had been their dog too.

Connor said, 'But you didn't kill Monty, remember?'

So I said, 'Okay. I'm sorry for leaving the gate open.'

Then Connor hit me on the arm and said, 'Just don't do it again.'

And we all laughed because the gate's open all the time now. There's no reason to shut it.

It was good to feel normal for once, but I hadn't forgotten about Splash. I kept thinking about her scales falling off. Maybe I'd kept her in a bucket too long. She needed to go back to the river. That was the only right thing to do.

I wished that I hadn't lied about Splash and kept her secret. I had thought I was protecting her, but now no one knew how special she was.

When I asked Dad if he would drive me and Splash down to the Oakdale River, he said that I could have the day off school tomorrow to think about Monty and take Splash to the river. Dad's not that bad, really.

When I went to bed that night, I gave Splash some worms and changed her water. She didn't look any worse than before. I wished she could talk. I wanted to ask her about her magic. Did it survive for only a short time? Why didn't it last forever?

'Tomorrow, we'll take you back to the river,' I whispered. 'You can have a normal home.'

I thought Splash might be too tired to listen to what I'd said, but she had heard. I didn't know it yet, but Splash had no plans to go back to the river.

12

At dawn the next morning I was woken by something wet on my face. I opened my eyes and wiped drops from my cheek.

In the dim light I saw scales flash in the air beside my bed, then disappear with a plop. I sat up and yawned. Splash was swishing in the bucket, facing my desk. When she saw me looking, she flipped her tail, as if she was pointing at something.

'What do you want, Splash?' I whispered. The apple-tree stick was still sitting on my desk. I picked it up. 'Do you want this?'

When Splash saw me pick up the stick, she turned in the bucket to face the door.

'Okay,' I said, 'if that's what you want.' With the bucket in one hand and the stick in the other I walked into the hall and stopped.

Splash, in her bucket, turned to face the

kitchen. When we got to the kitchen, Splash turned around to face the back door.

'Outside?'

As soon as we were out in the backyard Splash turned to face Monty's grave. I dared not hope.

I set the bucket down near the grave. Splash glistened in the morning sunlight but the dull patches where her scales had fallen off were bigger.

'Can you do it now, Splash?' I asked breathlessly. 'Can you bring back Monty?'

Her fins wilted. This wasn't the happy fish that I was so used to seeing.

'It's okay, Splash,' I said. 'Everything's alright. I feel better about Monty now. It's okay. Are you hungry?' The spot where Connor dug up his worms was right next to Monty's grave. It didn't take me long to dig up a worm for Splash.

When I held it in front of her face, she balanced it on her nose then tossed it to catch in her mouth.

'Wow!' That was impressive. It reminded me of Monty eating cheese.

I looked at the spot where Connor dug up

worms and then to Monty's grave. The faint
glimmer of an idea took shape inside me.

Splash had eaten worms from Monty's grave,
not just after she'd re-formed, but also when she'd
first been caught. The bait worms that Connor sold
to the cafe owner were from here. Was this where
the magic had begun? From a spark of something
still vital in Monty? Not his spirit exactly, but still
part of him . . . a memory of who he used to be.

It made me feel happy and sad all over again
to think that part of Monty had made his way
back to me . . .

Splash jumped out of the water and touched
her nose against Monty's apple-tree stick. When
I held it near her face again she pushed it towards
Monty's grave. There was still a small hole in it
from where I'd been digging the day before.

'Good idea.' I buried the roots of the stick in
the hole above Monty's grave.

I stood back, brushing soil from my hands.
'Okay now?' I asked Splash.

But her fins wilted even more.

Looking at Splash was like looking into a
mirror of my feelings for Monty. It was as if

Splash knew what I had been going through. She could understand how I felt.

Of course she could, something of Monty was in her . . .

I knelt next to the bucket. When she saw me kneel close, Splash jumped out of the bucket and touched my cheek with a kiss that felt like butterfly wings.

'I'm taking you back to the river. You should go home.'

But Splash kept pointing her face to Monty's grave.

'Do you mean . . .?' I whispered, not wanting to say it. 'Are we saying goodbye?' I was only just managing to let go of Monty. I didn't want to say goodbye to Splash too.

But Splash jumped again and gave me another soft kiss.

A lump formed in my throat as I realised what she was giving me – a chance to say that I was sorry. A chance to say goodbye.

Slowly, I nodded. 'Splash, I'll never forget you,' I said. 'Thank you.'

Splash flicked her tail happily in the water.

She didn't look sad now. She looked like she was ready to go.

'Goodbye, Splash,' I whispered.

Splash jumped out of the bucket and flopped onto the upturned soil. She lay next to the stick and lifted her face to look at me.

Then she lay still.

13

It happened in an instant. At first I could see the life in Splash, in her gills and in her body. Then she was gone. Her body lay still. Lifeless.

Soon her fins and her scales and her other features melted away until Splash became the fishy blob that had once floated in the bucket. The big piece separated into a pile of smaller slivers of trout. I remembered them flipping around my room. Now they lay drying out in the sun.

All that life and joy, all gone.

Using my hands as a scoop, I pushed dirt over the pieces of trout until they were buried beside the stick. Then I poured the water from Splash's bucket onto the mound of dirt. I imagined it trickling past the pieces of fish and the roots of the stick, then soaking further down to where Monty's body lay.

This was what Splash wanted. This was what she had asked me to do. This was why she had come.

I heard a noise behind me.

'Jamie!' It was Connor. And not just Connor; Mum and Dad were with him. 'Come and look,' I said, pointing at the little stick.

All three of them came and stood near Monty's grave. Mum put her arm around me. 'Are you okay, Jamie?' she asked.

'What do you think?' I began to say, but I didn't get any further.

Mum and Dad gasped as the stick started to push up. Thicker and taller it grew, as if we were watching it in time-lapse. When it was about as wide as my arm the trunk sprouted branches.

'Look at *that* . . .' cried Connor.

All four of us stepped back as the tree grew even more. It was my height and branching out. Clumps of dirt dropped away as the trunk pushed the soil aside. Twigs sprouted out of the branches. Leaves sprouted out of the twigs.

We stepped back again. The trunk grew thicker and thicker as the branches sprouted more and more twigs, and more leaves.

Finally we moved back one last time. In front of us stood a mature apple tree. Solid, strong.

'Oh my . . .' Mum whispered.

Before anyone else could speak, the tree blossomed.

Delicate, pale pink flowers appeared like fairy dresses. For a moment, they fluttered in the breeze. Then their centres swelled and grew into apples.

The apples grew bigger, riper, redder until the tree was covered.

Finally, one last branch reached out towards me and stopped just where I could touch it. A perfect apple dangled from the branch.

I reached out and picked the apple. Then I took a bite. The apple was sweet and juicy.

'Yum,' I said, and smiled at my family.

Connor was shaking his head in wonder. He looked as if he wanted to pick an apple too. But Mum and Dad looked stunned.

'Pick one, Connor,' I said. 'It's a present.'

Connor reached out and picked an apple. He paused for a moment then took a bite.

'Mmmmmm,' he munched. 'A present from who?'

'From Monty,' I said, 'and from Splash.'

The apple tree is still in our backyard. Its apples are the best I've ever tasted. And even though I've eaten dozens of apples now, I always think of Monty as I munch. The way he'd bound after a stick and then trot back happily with his ears pricked up. The way he used to make me feel. I think about Monty a lot, but I think about Splash too.

Even though she was only here a short time, I remember the clever jumps Splash made after she had done some magic, and the feeling of having something special to look after. When I go to the

Big Cow Cafe, I feel somehow close to her, even though she's gone.

I also remember the things she taught me, about life, and about death. About where things come from, like Monty's collar, and about where everything is going.

I miss Splash, but in the end, I know that she had to go. Even though she was magic, she wasn't meant to be here forever. Nothing is.

But I'll never forget.

1

'WOW, PRETTY COOL.'

'You can't even see the top.'

'Look at the size of that crane on the roof.'

Everyone around me has their heads back and their mouths open, staring up at Grand Southern Tower.

Not me. I keep my eyes locked on the ground. And my mouth shut.

'Alright, class,' calls Mr Tan. 'Pair up please. Find an excursion buddy.'

Voom. Even lightning doesn't move as fast as my class picking partners. Indigo is left with a choice between me and Big Mouth Bruce. She rubs her cheek and steps towards Bruce. Of course.

'Okaaay,' says Mr Tan looking at me. He's a relief teacher, so he's the only one who doesn't know what's going on. 'Do you want to form a group of three?'

I shake my head. 'No. See, I'm not actually going up. I'll just wait for you all down here.' I cross my arms to show that I'm the kind of person who means business. The decision has been made.

Mr Tan's eyes narrow. 'You're Alice, aren't you? Your mum called the school about this.'

'And explained why I won't be going up?' I ask hopefully.

'Actually, she thought it would be good for you, and I have to say that I agree.'

Great. That's all I need. Mum also thinks that broccoli and fresh air are good for me, so there's no trusting her judgement.

Mr Tan bends down until his face is level with mine, his hands on his knees. There's something about his eyes that makes it hard for me to look away. They're the blackest of any black that I've ever seen.

'Listen, Alice,' he says quietly. 'I know it's no fun being afraid. But if you face up to your fears, I promise you'll find they're not as bad as you think.'

Now he's sounding like Dad. *There is nothing to fear but fear itself.*

'I don't know,' I say slowly. 'Mrs Summers just lets me sit out.'

'Well, Mrs Summers isn't here now, is she?' Mr Tan smiles, and for a moment it's almost as if we're sharing our own private joke. 'Just stick with me and I'll talk you through it, okay?'

'Yeah, maybe . . .' I say vaguely. As far as relief teachers go, Mr Tan's not all that bad. But those big black eyes aren't fooling me. My feet are staying firmly on the ground, thank you very much.

Our class files into the lobby of the Grand Southern Tower. A huge banner reads GRAND OPENING! SEE THE CITY FROM THE TALLEST BUILD-ING IN THE SOUTHERN HEMISPHERE!

The ceiling's really high and hung with lights that look like huge snowflakes. Beyond the ticket booth is a whole row of lifts. As long as I don't go anywhere near them, I'll be fine.

Everyone's desperate to get to the lifts, but Mr Tan smiles and points us towards a sign that says INTERACTIVE CENTRE. 'How about we learn a bit about the structure before we go up, eh?'

Sounds good to me.

It's dark in the Interactive Centre, and the ceiling is low. I like it as soon as I step inside. Photos along one wall show every stage of the building process as well as the architecture plans. Scale models of other tall buildings around the world are roped off in the centre of the room. Dubai, New York, Taipei . . .

Shanghai has the highest outdoor observation deck in the world. I'm *definitely* not going to Shanghai. Ever. What if someone makes me go up and observe things?

When we come to the model of Grand Southern Tower, my eyes travel to the observation deck. They have to travel *up*. Even when it's just a model, this building is *taller* than me. That can't be healthy. I hold onto the rope and let my eyes drop down the length of the model. Floor after floor, all the way down to street level. Tiny little plastic people are frozen in position, going about their tiny little plastic lives . . .

The next thing I know, the room begins to tilt. My throat tightens and my knuckles turn pale as I clutch the rope.

'Impressive, hey?' Mr Tan juts his chin at the model of Grand Southern Tower. 'Cutting-edge engineering. It's safer than some buildings that are a tenth of this height.'

'It's not like I'm worried about the building falling down,' I say, turning away from the model.

Mr Tan's quiet, waiting. Even in the dim light I can feel him watching me.

So I take a breath and keep going. 'It's just . . . I get dizzy . . . My whole body goes weak and I have to grab onto something.' Like my excursion buddy, which is what happened last year when our class went on a trek to Maidenhair Falls. I look up at Mr Tan and hit him with my big guns. 'Then I start feeling *really* sick. You don't want me to throw up all over the floor, do you?' Or all over my excursion buddy which, unfortunately for Indigo, is also what happened last year at Maidenhair Falls.

Mr Tan laughs. 'No, I don't want that to happen. But if you face your fears today, I promise everything will be alright. Will you do that for me, Alice? Will you give it a shot?'

This is making me nervous. Mr Tan seems to have me at the top of his to-do list. The very top.

He leans close. 'Trust me, Alice. I used to be afraid of heights, too. But then something happened and I realised you can't run away from your fears forever.'

I swallow and nod because he's given me an idea. I'm going to run right outta here.

The tour guide taps Mr Tan on the shoulder and pulls him aside. It gives me a chance to scan the exits. The main archway where we entered the Interactive Centre is also the way you're meant to leave. But I see a door near the back of the room that looks promising. I'm too far away to read the sign.

Mr Tan glances in my direction then back to the tour guide, so I wander up to the other end of the room, pretending to be totally transfixed by the exhibits along the way.

When I casually glance back, Mr Tan is still talking to the tour guide, holding his arms out and shaking his head. Time to make my move. Indigo looks over as I pass, but I just smile and keep going. I'm not even sure what I'll do when I get through the door. Curl up in a dark corner? Find a broom closet and hide inside until the trip to the top is over? It's not like I want to run away, exactly. More like lie low until the storm clouds pass.

But when I reach the door, my heart sinks. THROUGH TO STAFF ELEVATORS, says the sign.

No way, I'm not going anywhere near those things. I spin around, looking for somewhere else to hide. In a little alcove in the corner I see a door I'd overlooked before, probably because it's painted all black. I can tell that it's not meant for the public. It almost seems to disappear into the wall.

I check to see if anyone's watching and just make out the top of Mr Tan's head moving through the crowd, turning from side to side as if he's looking for someone. Me?

He's tried so hard to help. I feel bad for sneaking away. For a moment Mr Tan's words come back. *You can't run away from your fears forever.*

I look at the door, then at the top of Mr Tan's head. It's stopped moving now, and is facing my way. I'm not sure if he can see me, it's so dim in here. But it makes me wonder, maybe I should stay ... Maybe I will be alright ...

Then I imagine what it would be like at the top of this place, teetering above the world and feeling like I'm about to fall off. What was I thinking? There's no way I'm going up the tallest building in the southern hemisphere. If people were meant to be that high, we'd have been born with jet engines.

I have to get out. Now! The knob on that strange black door seems to vibrate as I twist it, but the door doesn't budge. I take a breath and push against it with my shoulder. The door opens slightly with my weight and the hinges groan as if it hasn't been opened in ages. I keep pushing as hard as I can until the gap is wide enough for me to squeeze through.

As soon as the door clicks shut behind me my senses are filled with a low hum. It shakes my bones and makes my teeth vibrate. What is this place? It's a tiny room, close and enclosed. An eerie green glow lights up bare walls and another door a few steps away. I'm feeling around the room for a light switch when the humming stops. Just like that. All I can hear is the sound of my breathing. This place is creepy. There's no way I'm staying in here. But there's no way I'm going back into the Interactive Centre either. That leaves the other door.

As I push the door open, a breeze cools my skin. A breeze *inside* a building? Weird.

But that doesn't stop me from stepping through.

3

For some reason one ear blocks as soon as I'm through the door. Then the other does. I force a yawn until they both pop, sort of. I'm in a long corridor with doors along either side. Hotel rooms? Whatever they are, I don't think they're being used. There's no carpet on the floor. And the heating sure isn't on. It's freezing cold.

It's not until the door clicks shut behind me that I realise there's no way to open it from this side. It doesn't have a handle, just a rectangular seam. If I didn't know it was there, I wouldn't even realise it was a door.

Oh well, I don't want to go back into the Interactive Centre yet. I'll find another way back when I'm ready.

I hug my arms around my chest and wonder which way to go.

First, I try the nearest door. No luck. So

I start up the corridor. I'll find an empty room somewhere and wait it out for an hour or so. Once Mr Tan realises I'm missing, I'm sure he'll work out what's going on. He'll know that I just chickened out. He won't think I've been abducted or anything.

I round the corner at the end of the hall and a man in a hard hat and a tool belt clomps towards me. The echo of boots on the hard floor is the only sound. I walk towards him, head high, as if I'm meant to be here. Just a kid without a worry in the world.

When he comes close, the man stops and rubs his neck. 'What are you doing up here?'

'Me?' I flick a hand and keep walking. 'Just . . . ah . . . doing work experience with Mr Brunto-nelli . . .' Hope that sounds like someone's name.

I don't look back to see his reaction. I'm not sure where I'm going, but I'm going there as confidently as I can. Before turning the next corner, I stop and check the way I came. No hard hat following me. Good.

I slip round the corner to find a row of windows stretching the length of the corridor in front of me. They're tall and narrow, reaching almost to the floor.

As I look through the glass, a chill runs through me.

On the other side of the windows, just a few steps from me, is clear white sky.

Through the white I can just make out a hazy horizon, and below me, already spinning, are the tops of buildings.

Panic escapes my mouth as a squeak. I stumble away from the window, half-falling half-clambering backwards on hands and feet. Already the corridor is turning. I flip onto my stomach and cling to the floor as the whole world becomes a spinning vortex, slow at first then gaining speed.

Wherever I am, however I got here, I'm not on the ground anymore.

The world is a vortex and I'm going to fall off. I grip the floor with all I can. My heart hammers out of control. I have no idea how I came to be up here, but I can't think about that now. Breathing is pretty much all I can manage. Breathing and not throwing up.

My arms are weak, shaky, but I manage to crawl to the wall and rest a shoulder against it. The hardness of the floor is my lifeline.

Maybe the guy in the hard hat will come back this way. Or a new guy in a hard hat. Right now, I'd settle for an old woman in a sunhat. I'm not fussy. Over my racing heart, I listen for the sound of footsteps, but I can't hear any. No one knows where I am.

I'm not sure how long I stay sprawled on the floor, waiting for help. It's long enough for the spinning to slow. I concentrate on my breathing. Start thinking again.

At least, I think that's what I'm doing.

I have no idea how I came to be up here, but that doesn't worry me so much as how to get down again. I can't head back the way that I came. There's no way to open the door from this side.

At the end of the corridor I see a green sign marked with an arrow and the word ELEVATORS. I decide to follow. At least I haven't thrown up.

Concentrating on the floor, I begin to crawl towards the sign, sliding my shoulder along the wall. My arms are shaky. Small silver dots mark nails in the floor, and I find myself counting them, giving my mind something to think about.

Something other than where I am.

By the time I've counted to fifty-four I reach the corner. I'm feeling better now, light in the head but not as dizzy.

This hall is different from the others. It's even more cold and windy here. Windows still line one side, but stop at a gap in the middle. The lifts, I hope. I put my head down again and crawl forward. It's easier this time. My arms are stronger, and I actually feel like my breathing is under control.

When I judge that I'm close to where the lifts should be, I take a deep breath and look up.

It's a lift alright, but not the kind I was expecting. My stomach lurches as the sense of height hits me.

In front of me is a wire cage big enough to bring up building materials. It must be the worker's lift. It has a wooden floor. Diamond-shaped wire is the only thing that separates it from the open sky.

I push my shoulder hard into the wall, and let my head sink to the floor.

My only way down is to face the vortex.

But I can't do that. There's no way I'm getting in this lift with only bits of wire between me and the wide open sky. Only planks of wood stopping gravity from sucking me down. I don't care how long I have to stay up here. I'd rather die than ride in that thing. Maybe I'm *already* dead.

I check up and down the hall for more signs that might help me out of this. They all point this way. Maybe I'll go back to that weird old door and find a way through. I take a breath and start into a shuffling U-turn on all fours.

I'm halfway round when something in the lift catches my eye. A green, round button with an arrow beside it pointing to the floor. It's like a sign. A small piece of encouragement when I need it most.

It makes me think of Mr Tan and the way he tried to help me. The way he made it seem as if we were in this together. I can almost hear him encouraging me now.

You can't run away from your fears forever.

They're not as bad as you think.

I promise everything will be alright . . .

It's enough to make me stop. Wonder. Even from here I can feel the height, so much emptiness between that button and the ground. But if I could go in there I'll get down faster than any other way.

As soon as I start to see the possibility, something rises within me. Not the vortex yet, but a sense that maybe, somehow, I can do this.

The idea's inside me now. I don't want to back away. Still on all fours, I inch myself towards the lift. I'm not nervous now as much as curious. How close can I get before the world starts spinning? How much longer until my arms start to shake? I try not to think about the open space just beyond the lift but I can feel it swirling. Waiting to pull at me.

I'm about two metres away from the lift when I see a gap between the edge of the floor and the lift. It's only a few centimetres but beyond it, I feel so much space.

So much height.

It hits me like a ten-metre wave, lifting up my strength and tossing it away, leaving me tumbling, twirling, turning. Lost in the vortex again. My whole body's weak by the time I start thinking again. I feel sick to my core. But something has changed. Something is different now.

I've come too far to let this get the better of me. I'm not going to run away. As long as I can move, I'm moving forwards.

6

It's like stepping out of my body, leaving the fear behind. I place a hand on the wooden floor of the lift. It holds my weight without budging. At least there are no gaps in the wood. I pull a knee forward. Hand then knee . . .

I can hardly believe I'm here in the lift. No one else would believe it either. Especially not Indigo. I'm not myself anymore. I'm braver than I was.

Somehow, it's easier now, even though the breeze is still blowing. I'm in the lift and I'm still okay.

I can't reach the down button from my crouched position. So I lift my hands from the ground, kneel tall and bang the green button with my fist before I can think about what I've done.

The doors close and the lift lurches. I hug my

knees for dear life, scrunching my eyes shut and waiting for the world to start spinning.

But it doesn't. The only movement I feel is a slow, steady downward one. I gather my last shred of courage and open my eyes. On the other side of the wire the city sprawls before me. The world seems so simple from up here. So neat. It's the first time I've seen anything like it. Cars move like beetles through a maze of streets. People trail along like ants. That's my world down there, my life.

Beeping sounds as I near the ground. The lift clunks to a stops and the door slides open to reveal two fat men in hard hats carrying what looks like a shower screen.

'What you doing in here?' one of them asks.

I'm not sure how to answer that, so I don't. On hands and knees, I pad out onto the ground. Sweet, solid, stable ground. The concrete smells like sawdust.

'Hey, kid, you alright?' The two guys stare at me with their mouths open.

'I am now!' I stand up and brush the dirt off my hands.

I pull myself together and stride around the side of the building, not looking back to see if they're still staring.

It's not until I've made it to the front of Grand Southern Towers that I stop. With one hand against the wall, I look up. I can't even see the top, but I know I was up there only minutes ago. I can't believe that just happened. I can't believe I'm still alive.

I faced the vortex and survived.

Now I just have to face my class. Maybe I'll be in time to go up again with them.

It couldn't be as bad as what I just went through. The public lifts will be enclosed so I know I can handle them. And the observation deck, well . . . At least that should have carpet on the floor if I feel the need to crawl.

My class won't believe it. And Mr Tan. He'll get a real surprise.

I stride across the lobby to the bank of lifts. But there's nobody there. Maybe they've gone up already? I'm trying to summon the courage to face the lift alone when I hear a familiar voice behind me.

It's Mr Tan. He has his back to me and is waving his hands as if he's a traffic controller and our class is a jumbo jet. I'm surprised that they're only just coming out of the Interactive Centre. It felt as if I was up the top for years.

I duck behind a pillar and manage to join the tail-end of our group without Mr Tan noticing. Everyone's walking slowly, with their shoulders slumped. Big Mouth Bruce is dragging his feet, not saying anything for once.

Indigo turns to me and sighs, 'Well, at least *you're* happy, Alice.'

Me, happy? Traumatised maybe. And a whole lot relieved. As far as I can tell, no one seems to have noticed that I was missing.

Before I can ask Indigo why I should be happy, Mr Tan comes close and fixes his black eyes on me. 'Well, Alice, I guess you're off the hook this time. You'll have to face your fears some other day.'

'What do you mean *some other day*?' I blurt out. I don't care how strange it sounds.

'Wake up, Alice,' says Indigo. 'The public lifts are broken. So no one's going up.'

It takes a while for her words to sink in. No one's going up? I just stand there spluttering. I'm not sure if I want to cheer or scream. If I'd stayed with my class and not snuck away, then I never would have left the ground?

Mr Tan watches my reaction, a small smile on his lips. 'I don't think the day's been a complete waste, though,' he says.

Even though I want to look away, I can't.

'I'm proud that you didn't run from your fears, Alice. That's the first step in dealing with them. Wouldn't you agree?'

And then, he winks.

NIGHT SIGHT

1

WE TAKE THE CORNER SO FAST that my shoulder bumps against the door. I'm pinned back in my seat as Dad accelerates.

'Where are we going?' I say. 'The shops are the other way. What about the rolls for lunch?'

'Making ... a slight ... change of plans,' mutters Dad between gear changes.

Oh no. Not again. I should have stayed at home.

We're swerving in and out of traffic like they do in the movies; I just grip the doorhandle and wait to see what happens next.

It's not going to be boring, at least I know that much. My dad does stuff like this all the time. Well, not the stunt-car driving, I mean the sudden change of plans.

Usually his craziness is more weird than dangerous – like the time Mum brought take-away noodles home and Dad threw the whole lot straight into the bin. Or the time my class was going to the zoo. Dad took one look at the bus driver and insisted on driving me himself. I'll never live that one down.

But that's not the worst thing he's done.

When I was eight and we were at the park, Dad saw this kid who was there on his own and decided to give him my bike. Just like that. Helmet and everything.

He. Gave. My bike. Away.

It didn't matter that he bought me another bike the next day. By then, the damage had been done. I even tried dialling triple zero to report a case of child abuse, but Mum stopped me before I could explain to the lady on the other end of the phone what it was like having a loopy dad.

Whenever I complain to Mum she just sighs

and smiles. *I know he's hard to understand, Danny, but he means well . . .*

Which is another way of saying that I just have to live with it.

As long as I don't die right now in a fiery car crash, that is! Dad might be well-meaning, but he sure isn't a stunt-car driver. He overtakes a car right in front of a truck coming the other way.

We're going to crash. 'Dad, what are you *DOING*?' I scream.

We just make it back to our side of the road as the truck flies past with its horn blaring. 'All under . . . control,' pants Dad, and changes gears again.

Yeah right.

The only thing ahead of us now is a big hippy van. Dad plants his foot. The van makes it through a set of lights just as they change to amber. Dad swears.

For scary seconds we keep flying forwards and my heart thumps HIT THE BRAKES in Morse code. I grip the handle on the door and plant my feet into the floor because I'm sure we're about to crash. We're flying at eighty kilometres an hour towards a set of red lights.

At the very last minute, Dad does hit the brakes and we screech to a jolting stop. The bonnet of our car is poking out onto the pedestrian crossing. People peer in at us as they pass. I pretend not to notice.

Dad turns to me and jiggles my seatbelt buckle.

'All secure, Danny?' he asks. 'No twists in the belt?'

I don't like the sound of that.

He revs the engine like a crazed petrolhead. The lights change, and we're off like a rocket. We're ahead of the pack now and speeding down a clear, straight road.

Soon we reach the hippy van. It has flowers and psychedelic swirls all over it. Even its windows are painted. Dad overtakes it easily so I'm totally unprepared for what happens next.

As Dad hits the brakes again, my seatbelt jerks tight and it's suddenly hard to breathe. Our car is screaming to a stop, and I hear a different screech coming from the hippy van behind us. Then . . .

Crunch. We jerk forwards with the sound of tearing metal.

The next thing I know, everything is white.

2

Where am I? My arms are pinned down by a giant marshmallow. For a moment I think I'm going to drown in puff. Then I realise what's happened. It's the airbag.

Dad pushes it away from my face. 'Danny, are you okay?'

I'm fine. No thanks to you, is what I want to say. But I just nod and keep my mouth shut because if I open it, I know I'll start yelling.

Dad checks over his shoulder at the van jammed into the back of our car. He pulls out his mobile, fighting against his own airbag, and presses triple zero.

'Yes,' says Dad. 'There's been an accident on the corner of Hampton and Station Streets.'

The airbags have deflated enough for us to get out of the car. I feel sick when I see the crumpled metal and broken tail-lights scattered across the road. It's hard to see the hippies inside their van because of the painted windows and shattered windscreen, and I start to worry that someone might be really hurt in there.

People have gathered around to help. At least two of them are talking on their mobiles.

'You okay?' asks a man, rushing up to us. He doesn't wait for an answer, but keeps going straight for the van and tugs one of the doorhandles. The door doesn't budge.

Dad puts both hands on my shoulders and steers me towards a bus shelter. But before we get there I hear the revving of an engine and we turn to see the hippy van's wheels spinning up clouds of smoke. The driver must be trying to reverse away from our car. At least that means they're okay. They're not going anywhere, though, because the front of their van is snagged on the back of our car.

'Wait here, Danny,' says Dad, and pushes me into the bus shelter. 'Don't come out until the police get here.'

'Hold on. But, *what are you doing . . .*' I pull

away and glare at him. This is all his fault, and, as far as I can tell, the dangerous part is all over now anyway . . . *or didn't you notice, Dad?*

He holds my shoulders and looks into my eyes. 'Promise me, Danny. What did I say?'

I keep glaring because I don't want him thinking he's got away with any of this. Mum's not going to take his side on this one.

'Promise me, Danny,' says Dad again, and checks over his shoulder.

I roll my eyes. 'Okay. I won't move until the police come.'

'Great. Okay, good,' says Dad and disappears.

I sit down on the bench in the shelter and check myself for blood and broken bones. Anything that might count as proof when I report this as child abuse. I don't even find a scratch. Pity.

I'm so sick of the weird stuff my dad does. He's the one who caused all the trouble and now he thinks that just calling the police will fix everything. But from what I've learnt about the police in the past week, it's a mistake to expect any help from *them*.

I stand up and check out the accident scene, but it's just a whole bunch of people standing around doing nothing, so I sit back down.

So much for fresh bread rolls. Now I have to sit here in this bus shelter, waiting for the police to show up. Why does weird stuff always happen to me? In some ways I'm not as freaked out by all this as I might have been. It's not half as strange as the other stuff that's been happening these past weeks.

I haven't told anyone what's been going on, so it's good to have a chance to think it through. I settle in and let my mind drift back to the night of my thirteenth birthday.

That's the night my life changed forever.

As birthdays go, my thirteenth was a good one – a new racing bike, a movie with my mates and dinner at our family's favourite pasta place.

Dad had a bit too much red wine and kept asking me, 'Do you feel any different now that you're a teenager, Danny? My thirteenth birth-day was really big for me.'

'Nup, no different,' was my answer, no matter how many times he asked.

In the end my little sister Amber squeezed my arm and giggled, 'He feels like a teenager to me, Dad!'

By the time I got to bed I was really tired, weighed down with lasagne and two pieces of blackforest cake with ice-cream. I must have fallen asleep straight away, because I woke up later with a head full of dreams. I rolled over and tucked my pillow under my chin the way I like it. The next thing I knew I was dreaming again . . .

I was looking down at my bed from above, looking at *myself* lying in bed – arm out of the doona, pillow tucked just so . . . I'd never seen myself in a dream before and the detail freaked me out – my hair kinked up at the back, my chest moving slowly. It was so *real*.

I watched my sleeping self roll over . . . and the next thing I knew I was awake, lying on my back in bed, and feeling just a tad spooked.

I'd had my fair share of unsettling dreams, of course – teeth falling out or being stuck in the mud, for example. Sometimes I even got to fly really close to the ground, a bit like surfing one metre off the grass. But I'd never seen myself from the outside before.

It was the first time, but not, as it turned out, the last.

The next night I dreamed again that I was looking down at my sleeping self. But I could think more clearly than I usually could in dreams. And I noticed all the small details of the scene. A fly was rubbing its feet together on the windowsill. My doona was about to fall off the bed. The dictionary I'd spent ages searching for the week before was wedged between the back of my desk and the wall.

And even though I was in a dream fog, it suddenly hit me. I was *seeing* all this, not dreaming it. I was hovering above myself, looking at it all for real.

A realisation like that can really shock a person.

I wokeup, fighting with my doona, falling

out of bed, then crawling to look behind my desk.

Freak-out big time . . .

My Japanese dictionary was just where I'd seen it, between the back of my desk and the wall. Was it possible that I'd noticed the dictionary some other time, and this had just been a dream? I didn't think so. As weird as it seemed, it felt *real*.

I didn't sleep much that night.

When I tried looking it up on the internet the next day, I wasn't sure what to type in. *Dreaming real things* brought up a whole heap of music lyrics, and *looking at yourself when you're asleep* found pages to do with 'looking after yourself'. At first.

As I kept scrolling, strange new words began to appear: *astral projection, lucid dreaming, out of body experiences . . .*

There were words to describe what had been happening to me.

In fact, there weren't just words to describe my strange dreams, there were whole chat forums about whether or not it was possible. There were heaps of books on the subject.

The internet is an amazing place. There were even sites explaining how to make it happen and what to expect.

As you fall asleep, picture yourself in the place you'd like to reach. There's no danger in astral projection. If you wake up, you will simply return to your body.

By the time I went to bed the next night, I was all set and ready to astral project outside, not just in my room.

Once I'd decided I wanted to do that, it was easy as a piece of pie. All I had to do was think *I'm going outside tonight.*

I brushed my teeth, pulled on my pyjama shorts and snuggled into bed. Then I pulled my pillow under my chin, shut my eyes and started to drift . . .

The next thing I knew, there I was.

Hovering in our front yard.

It wasn't like flying or floating or anything like that because my body wasn't there to feel. It stayed warm and snug, with the pillow tucked under its chin, while the rest of me got to go outside. A banksia bush in our front yard rustled slightly in the breeze. Its reds and brown-greens looked almost monochrome in the moonlight.

As far as banksia bushes go, that one was nothing special. But I'll never forget what it looked like because *seeing* it like that meant I'd been given a whole new life – *bonus* time. I didn't have to be scared of falling, or worry I'd get cold. I didn't have to tell Mum and Dad what I was doing.

At that moment, I felt like the luckiest kid ever.

The world was out there, just waiting for me to explore.

I used to think the whole world shut down at night, as if my parents turning out their lights made everything go black and silent. How wrong I was.

Even on my first night when I just hung out in our street, I saw more happening than I'd expected. It was fun to see a fat possum clambering along branches and telephone wires – Possum King of the night. The guy who lives at the end of our street came home late, with food stains down his front and sweat circles under his arms. He took his dog out into the yard. It took ages sniffing and scratching around in the cold, but the guy just stood there yawning and rubbing his forearms, talking softly to it.

The next night I explored a bit further and popped in to see my friend Heath. He was asleep with his head half off the bed and his arms outstretched as if he was flying.

The night after that I got really excited and decided to try for the moon. If my body wasn't coming with me, then it didn't matter that there wouldn't be any air to breathe. I was really disappointed when I always found myself in our backyard, no matter how many times I tried. I'd snuggle into bed picturing myself on the moon. My limbs would relax, my mind would drift . . .

The next thing I knew, I would be looking at those banksia flowers. Again.

In the end I decided that I had to stick to

places that were familiar. I'd never been to the moon before, so maybe I had no link to project myself there.

In fact, I found it hard to control where I went even when I knew the place well. One night I tried to go exploring at school but ended up at Mr Eriksson's house. He was watching a movie with Miss Withers. Who would have guessed they were a couple? She had her hair out of a bun, and her legs resting on Mr Eriksson's lap. She looked way younger than normal.

I didn't tell anyone what I'd seen, not even Heath. It felt too private. Watching someone who doesn't know they're being watched is almost like seeing them, well, naked. You see all the secrets they try to hide.

The guy in the suit had me stumped for a while. He just looked like your average businessman, except he was searching through a rubbish bin when I first saw him. Maybe he'd had a fight with his girlfriend, I thought, and in a fit of fury she'd thrown an expensive necklace away. Or maybe he'd lost some important business documents and millions of dollars were at stake.

As I kept watching, though, he pulled out an old takeaway container. He lifted the lid and sniffed. The next thing I knew, he had torn off a bit of cardboard and was using that as a spoon.

Talk about an unusual business dinner.

If I'd had my stomach with me, it would have been churning. He was eating the way dogs do – swallowing without really chewing. From the way he kept checking up and down the street I could tell that he didn't want anyone to see him.

When he was finished, he dropped everything back in the bin, brushed off his hands, and headed down the street looking once again like an everyday businessman. Except I had a feeling he wasn't going home to a nice warm bed.

I went straight home to my own warm bed after that.

In fact, most nights I only explored for an hour or so before returning to my body, glad to have a warm doona to pull up and a family asleep just down the hall. It felt somehow lonely to be out there, exploring the night world.

And, I have to admit, some of the time it was worse than lonely. Sometimes it was scary.

It's hard to explain, but once or twice a feeling came over me as if someone else was with me. Not someone I could see, but something ... else. A kind of presence. One minute I'd be drifting over a street or in someone's house and the next I'd have to turn around, expecting to see someone ...

Or something.

Not that I believe in ghosts or anything like that, but that sense of *something else* still made me think about spirits and guardian angels ...

I hoped it wasn't something worse.

Two weeks after my thirteenth birthday I saw something that I'd never seen before, something I came to wish I *hadn't* seen.

It was a dark night without much moonlight. I was exploring the streets past the paper mill.

Even though it was just row after row of old houses, it was still fun to explore. I felt a bit like Superman, flying over it all.

I saw a rhododendron bush shake by the side of a house and drew closer to see if it was a dog or a possum. When I managed to get a clear view from above the bush, though, I realised that it wasn't an animal making the bush shake, it was a TV. If I could have giggled out loud, I would have, because the TV seemed to hover in the air as it moved past the bush.

Once the TV came out from behind the rhododendron, I realised it wasn't hovering. It was being carried by two men. I hadn't seen them at first because they were both wearing black jackets. Even their faces were dark because they both had beards.

I could hear them whispering as they man-oeuvred the TV into the back of a truck.

There was a loud crash.

'What are you doing, Bob?' snapped one of the men.

'Spiders. I hate 'em,' said Bob.

The other guy snorted. 'Well, be quiet about it, alright!'

Weird time of night to be moving house, was my first thought. It wasn't until the two men went back into the house and came out with two speakers and a laptop that I started to think it through. Two guys, working *at night*, moving only electronic stuff . . . which was *easy to sell.*

The next thing I knew I was in bed, shocked awake and gasping. Somewhere on the other side of town, those two guys were stealing from that house. I felt dirty to have seen them, as well as angry and scared.

I slid out of bed and down the hall. It was pretty dark. I ran my hand along the wall as I walked, to be sure of where I was. For all I knew, people could be asleep in that house. What if they woke up? What if the burglars had guns?

Mum had a list of emergency numbers in the kitchen – poisons information, fire brigade, police. I grabbed the phone, listened for a dial tone and punched in the number for our local police station. Even though it was an emergency, I thought our local police would be better than triple zero. They were closer and there wasn't much time.

'There's a robbery happening, right now!' I cried as soon as someone answered the phone.

'What's your location?' came a deep voice.

'It's out past the paper mill . . .' I counted in my head. 'Five, maybe six streets past it, I think. There are two guys loading stuff into a truck.'

The police officer cleared his throat. 'And where are *you* calling from?'

'I'm at home,' I said. 'But that's not important—'

'Can I speak to your parents, please?'

I got it then. He thought I was playing a prank. 'No. They're asleep. But I'm not joking, sir. There really is a robbery going on.'

'Okay,' said the police officer slowly. 'Tell me exactly what you saw.'

'Two guys carrying a big TV out of a house, and other stuff too. Just send out a car and you'll find them. It's a big white truck.'

'And what's the address of the house being robbed?'

'I . . . I'm not sure,' I said, thinking fast. 'I'm a

sleepwalker, see, and I was out sleepwalking . . . when I woke up I saw it all.'

'Dangerous habit, son,' said the police officer. 'Where *exactly* do you live?'

Inside I groaned, because my real address wouldn't make sense if I'd been sleepwalking. I live on the other side of town. It was the kind of hole in my story that the police officer was looking for.

For a second I thought about making up an address using one of the street names from out past the mill. But after some brain crunching – Andrew St? Anderson St? Amsterdam? – I realised there wasn't going to be any police sirens screaming out past the mill that night.

I sighed. 'Never mind. Sorry,' I said, and hung up.

I didn't sleep much for the rest of that night. Even though I tried to astral project again, I kept waking up back in my bed.

Somewhere out there, two guys were sneaking away with other people's stuff. And no one was going to stop them.

6

The next day after school, I rode my bike out past the paper mill.

Two streets along, I was lost. I'd expected to find the house in a flash, but riding a bike was totally different from astral projecting. Everything looked so different from the ground. Everything *felt* so different during the day.

I could remember a wattle tree in the second street, then a couple of clean red roofs. For a while I felt as if I was chasing my own tail – looking for a tree that seemed to move whenever I came near it.

Eventually I found the wattle tree *four* streets along, not two. And I was eight streets along by the time I found the house that had been robbed. I wrote down the address of the house – 23 Andrews Ave – and headed back into town to the police station.

My legs were aching, but I was on a mission.

It was too late to stop the robbery, of course, but I still had information that might help catch the thieves. Maybe the police would recognise them from my description and would be able to bring them straight in for questioning.

A man and woman were standing at the reception bench of the station, talking really fast to a police officer. It would have been pretty awesome if they'd been the people who had been robbed. I'd just step up and cool-as-you-please give them the information that they needed. But after hearing a few sentences I realised they were talking about their next-door neighbour and a broken fence.

I stood and waited.

Past the reception desk, another police officer was typing at a computer. After a while she glanced up, sighed and typed a bit more. Then she stood up and came to the bench.

'Can I help you?'

'Yes, I have some information about a burglary.'

I'd barely got the words out when she pushed a clipboard over the counter at me.

'Fill this out please,' she said before returning to her seat.

Property Theft Report was written at the top of the page. I was glad I'd found out the address of the house that had been robbed, because it was one of the first questions. But the rest of the page asked questions that I couldn't answer – means of entry, insurance company, items stolen. Even when I flipped over the page, there was nowhere to fill in 'description of thieves' or 'type of getaway vehicle'.

When the couple had left, I cleared my throat and looked at the first police officer. 'Ah, excuse me, has a robbery been reported for a house on Andrews Avenue?'

'Sorry, I can't give away information like that.'

'Well, see, I saw the robbers, so I need to report what they look like.'

Before I knew it, there was another clipboard on the bench, but I wasn't about to give up. 'No . . . but see, there's nowhere to write what they look like or what kind of truck they were using, and I *saw* them.'

'Alright,' said the police officer with a slight shrug. 'What kind of truck was it?'

'Big!' I said, showing with my hand up high. 'And white, but old like ... a real bomb of a truck. And the thieves had leather jackets and bushy beards.'

The officer snorted and called over his shoulder. 'Hey, Sandy! Call in the Special Forces. We've got a lead.'

By now Sandy was leaning back in her chair, smiling and nodding. 'Is that so?'

'Yeah, we've had a sighting – two crims with *beards*.' The officer chuckled.

I let my hand drop. 'But ... isn't that the kind of stuff you need to know?'

When the officer saw the look on my face, he stopped laughing and sighed. He disappeared under the bench and then appeared again holding a pile of files. It was about as tall as a thirty-centimetre ruler.

'See all these?' he said. 'That's how many burglaries have been reported this month. And unless we catch the burglars with the stolen goods, there's nothing we can do about it.' He shook his head and sighed. 'Sorry, mate.'

That was the end of my great plan to catch the thieves, but I haven't stopped thinking about them. It makes my blood boil that they could steal stuff and not get caught.

I've tried astral projecting and looking for their secret hide-out or maybe catching them with their loot again. I managed to find their truck once, but it had been dumped in a wrecker's yard, which was no help.

I haven't been able to find anything else. It doesn't help that every time I astral project lately I find myself back in bed, annoyed and awake. It might be because I'm scared of what I'll see out there. Twice in the past week I've had a sense of something out there with me, like a spirit or something else. Mostly though, I think I'm scared of seeing things that shouldn't be happening . . . of not being able to stop them.

If I could think of a way, I'd do it in the blink of an eye.

7

I've been sitting at the bus stop for fifteen minutes when an ambulance roars past and stops beside the hippy van and our mangled car, but I don't go over to check it out. I'll wait here until the police turn up. Once they've dealt with the people in the van they might have a word to say to my dad about dangerous driving. Not to mention reckless parenting . . .

Finally, a police car shows up. It has the lights flashing, but no siren.

At last. I stand up and walk closer. Dad's in the crowd, talking to a woman as they watch what's going on. Firefighters are working on the hippy van, trying to open the door.

Part of me wants to go back to the bus shelter. I don't want to see anyone get pulled out if they're bloody and hurt. But at the same time, I can't look away.

As soon as the police officers get out of their car, I see it's the two I spoke to at the station. One walks up to a guy in a fire chief uniform while the other goes to help two firefighters working on the van. There's a bit of a crowd in front of the door when they finally prise it open, so for a few seconds I don't see the hippies.

Then two men climb out, and my mouth falls open.

They're not hippies. They're wearing leather jackets and they both have bushy beards . . .

It's the thieves!

I can't believe it. What are the chances? They don't seem hurt. In fact, they're looking around as if working out if they can bolt.

'Danny!' calls Dad. He points to the bus shelter.

No way. I dash over to the police officer who I spoke to at the station. 'Excuse me, sir—' I begin, but he holds up his hands.

'Sorry, kid,' he says. 'Stay back, please.' But then he looks at me properly and cocks his head, as if he remembers me.

'It's them, sir!' I whisper, pointing and nodding urgently. 'The thieves I was telling you about. You know, the ones with *beards* . . .'

The officer looks at the thieves and then back at me. 'You know, we did chase up a lead based on your description of the truck, but it was registered under a false name.'

To one side, I see Dad stop walking. He tilts his head and watches me.

'Look in *this* van.' I work hard to keep my voice quiet. 'I bet their loot is inside!'

The officer puts a hand to his hip and for a moment I think he's going to pull out a gun. My heart hammers.

Thank goodness, it's just a notebook. The officer nods once and walks over to the other officer before they both peer into the van.

The thieves frown at each other and their bodies tense. One says something and they both step back from the crowd.

Slowly, so no one will notice, the thieves walk away.

What can I do? Those guys are big and there's only one of me. I glance around, trying to think.

Dad's glaring at me but there's no time to explain. I can't let those thieves get away. Not after trying so hard to catch them. Not after seeing them steal that TV . . .

I think back to the night I first saw those thieves. It gives me an idea.

8

'Hey, Bob!' I call out. 'There's a spider on your back!'

I'm not even sure which one is Bob, but soon it's obvious. He's the one waving his arms around, turning in circles and yelling, 'Where? Where? Get it off!'

The other thief stops to look. And the police spring into action. Their handcuffs come out and they move fast, shouting orders at the thieves and taking command.

Those big guys and their beards are put into the police car and taken away.

Just like that the thieves have been caught. I can't believe my luck.

Dad walks over to me with a big grin on his face. He looks like he's just won the lottery, not totalled our car.

'All's well that ends well, eh, Danny?' he says and ruffles my hair. 'Good sometimes comes from bad.'

'Yeah, what are the chances?' I say. 'Those two thieves had all their loot in that van.'

'Really?' he says and smiles. 'Looks like it all turned out for the best. How about we get those fresh rolls before we catch a taxi home? I've given my number to the cops and the tow-truck driver. And I've already called Mum.'

'Ah . . . okay . . .' I say slowly. The way Dad's smiling, it almost seems like he expected this to all work out.

So we head off down the footpath. Just like that.

I keep looking at him as we walk. 'So, are you going to tell me what you were doing?' I ask eventually.

'Well, what do *you* think I was doing?' Dad asks.

'I don't know,' I grumble. It's bad enough having a crazy dad, but it's even worse when he doesn't admit that he was acting weird.

We find a bakery a few blocks away. Dad even buys us a couple of meat pies to eat on the way home.

After Dad calls a taxi, we wait on the corner. It's the middle of the afternoon by now. A family wanders past eating ice-cream and teasing each other about the football.

A bus pulls up and rumbles for a while before rolling away. I wonder why the man sitting at the bus stop doesn't get on.

He's wearing a business suit, and now that I look closer I can see creases on the arms and legs as if he's slept in it. I've seen this man before . . .

He's the one I saw when I was astral projecting, the one who was looking through rubbish bins for food. To everyone else he looks like a business-man waiting for the bus, but I know he's not.

'How about a meat pie while we wait, hey Danny?' says Dad.

'Yeah . . .' I mumble.

The meat pies smell like a feast.

I can't just stand around without doing something. I step towards the man. 'Excuse me, sir, do you want these?' I say. 'We bought too many.'

The man frowns at me.

'We don't need them. Really,' I say, and leave the bag beside him on the bench. He's looking hungrily at the bag as I turn away. I don't want to make a big deal about it. I head back to Dad, trying to work out how to explain why I just gave his meat pie away. He must think I've gone loopy.

'See, it's like this . . .' I begin. Then I bite my lip. 'It's hard to believe . . .'

'I know, Danny. No need to explain,' says Dad. He's smiling, and it's more than just a happy smile, it's proud and meaningful and understanding.

'You *know*?' I ask.

'Know what?' grins Dad with a wink.

A look passes between us as it finally sinks in. 'You know!' I say again, and now I'm grinning too.

Finally, it all makes sense. Not just the way Dad understands why I gave that man our meat pies, but all the other weird stuff he's done – causing the accident, giving my bike away, even throwing out the noodles. To everyone else those things seem crazy, but that's only because they haven't seen the things we have. They don't know the secrets people keep and the things they do when they think they're not being watched.

Suddenly I'm glad I came with Dad today. Maybe I'll hang out with him a bit more. We share a pretty big secret, after all.

The presence I feel on the astral plane is not a ghost or angels, it's even better.

It's my dad.

1

IT SEEMED LIKE A GOOD IDEA at the time.

Well . . . no. If I'm being completely honest, I thought it was a risky idea that no one was going to find out about. I guess it wasn't until I'd made it into the jeweller's that I really thought about the seriousness of what I was about to do.

The shop door jangled shut behind me and I blinked in the darkness. *Who turned out the lights?*

I blinked again.

The lights weren't out, they were just dim.

Hundreds of rings and pendants glimmered like fireflies in a cave.

I can still turn around, I thought. *If Mum and Dad find out what I'm doing they'll kill me.*

'Can I help you?' someone called from the back of the shop.

I gulped. My hand hovered over the bulge in my pocket. I glanced at the door behind me. At least no one from outside could see me. In the gloom I could just make out the shop owner standing behind the counter. He was bald and stubby, not much taller than me, with old-man-spectacles halfway down his nose.

'What can I do for you, young man?' he asked, resting his elbows on the counter.

I took a breath and stepped forward. 'The sign outside says "Jewellery bought and sold".' Using just my thumb and pointer finger I pulled a padded leather box from my pocket, laid it on the counter and pushed it towards the old man.

I didn't even like touching the box, let alone what was inside. For the past two weeks I'd kept it wrapped in a green shopping bag and jammed at the back of my wardrobe with last year's smelly sneakers.

The old man flipped the lid, picked up a magnifying glass and licked his lips.

I wanted to close my eyes or turn away, but I couldn't. I leaned forwards to see as the old man examined the watch. It was about the spookiest thing I'd ever seen.

It had a deep-blue face and a black circle in the centre where the hands were attached. It looked exactly like a staring eye. I tried to ignore the shiver creeping up my spine.

Only a month before, that watch had been on a withered wrist on the other side of the world – the withered wrist of my great-grandmother.

I'd never met my great-grandmother. I'd never even been to Greece. But when she died, all her belongings had been shared among her family around the world – her furniture to everyone in Greece, vases and artwork to family in the US, and for my family in Australia, the jewellery.

Dad was the only one in my family to inherit anything that wasn't jewellery – he got a worn-out recipe book. Not that he even knew how to cook. Mum always moans that neither of us help out in the kitchen.

The man looked up at me. 'Well, well, well,' he said. 'I assume you don't have a certificate of ownership?' He glanced at me as I shook my head, then back at the watch as if he didn't want to take his eyes off it for long. 'I think I can make an exception . . .'

Seeing him want the watch so badly almost gave me second thoughts, but deep down, I knew this was my only chance. If I didn't sell it now, I'd never be able to come up with a story that would cover me as good as this one.

There was no way I was letting that thing anywhere near *my* wrist. For all I knew, my great-grandmother had been wearing it when she died . . .

It was much better to sell the creepy thing so that some *still living* old lady could put it on *her* wrinkly wrist. That way, everyone would get something they wanted. It made complete sense.

The old man was breathing as if his nose were a wind instrument. 'I'll give you three hundred dollars,' he said slowly. 'I'll have to replace the band and, of course, spend time working on it.'

I bit my lip. That was enough for what I needed. But was it fair? For all I knew, the guy could be a total crook.

I shook my head. 'Three hundred dollars? It's worth way more than that,' I said, trying to sound tough.

The old man smiled. Or maybe he snarled. 'Think so, do you?' he said, looking over his spectacles. 'I can go as high as three hundred and fifty but that's my final offer.'

'Okay.' I tried to swallow. It was hard to breathe. The glowing pendants and rings seemed to be eyes, watching me.

Five minutes later, I was sliding into the front seat of our car, blinking in the sunlight.

'All done?' asked Mum.

'Yeah, thanks,' I said vaguely, but I could tell she was about to ask another question. 'Nothing worth buying, though,' I added. There was no way I was going to tell her what I'd done.

Mum nodded. 'No point wasting your hard-earned money, Tony.'

She could say that again!

My hand slid to the bulge of notes in my pocket. It was more money than I had ever owned. And I knew exactly what to do with it.

2

My sisters, Clio and Poppy, were standing at the front door when we got home. They were each wearing about two kilograms of make-up and their hair was wrapped up in towels.

'Did you get it?' they said at the same time, jiggling up and down like toddlers who need to go to the bathroom, except Poppy is fourteen and Clio is fifteen.

Mum held up two tubs of hair gel, and all three of them disappeared into the bathroom. The girls had callisthenics exams later that day, which was fine with me as it meant I could have climbed onto the roof yelling *Watch me fly*, and no one would have noticed. All part of my plan.

Dad wasn't going to be so easy to avoid though; I sucked in a breath when he walked out of the kitchen.

'Home from cricket already?' I said.

Dad held up a salami sandwich about the size of my head and grinned. 'You better believe it, sonny-boy.' Which meant his team had won. 'How did the garage sale go?' He held off taking another bite while he waited for my answer.

'Great!' I said, pulling the wad of notes out of my pocket.

Dad placed a hand on my shoulder. 'Well, good stuff. I'm proud of you, Tony.'

I developed a sudden fascination with a fly rubbing its wing together on the wall. The truth was, the garage sale had been a total flop.

The afternoon before, I'd sneezed my way through two hours of sorting out all the old stuff in the garage, looking for things to sell. In the morning I'd set everything up in the driveway and sat around *not* making a lot of money. Unless you call twelve dollars and seventy-five cents a lot of money. It turns out rusty old scooters and tatty magazines don't exactly pull in the big bucks.

'Earning money feels good, doesn't it, son?' said Dad. 'It feels a whole lot better than just getting life handed to you on a silver platter.'

He still had his hand on my shoulder as if we were sharing a big father–son moment.

'Yeah, Dad, you're so right,' I mumbled. Guilt flickered in my gut, but not for long.

This whole situation was Dad's fault anyway. Well, Mum's and Dad's. They think we live in the Dark Ages, or some other time before kids were allowed to have fun. We're not allowed to have any games that need batteries or a power socket. We're lucky to have a TV.

On its own this wouldn't exactly be the end of the world, I guess. Like, I'm a wiz with card tricks and I'm pretty good at climbing trees. But I have to live in the twenty-first century, with friends who live in the twenty-first century too. Nico and Andy play computer games *all the time*. And when they're not playing games, they're talking about playing games, while I stand around with nothing to say. Whenever I go round to Andy's place, I always end up dead or with a really low score because I'm not as good as they are.

Yeah, that's heaps of fun.

So over the holidays I ramped up the begging, and three weeks ago my parents finally gave in. They said I could have a game console. But there was a catch: I had to earn the money myself.

At first I was really excited, but I soon realised I'd entered a whole new world of torture. It was going to take *forever* to earn enough money. If I washed the car *every week for a year*, I'd still only have enough for the console itself, not any actual games. Those things cost heaps.

It wasn't until I found myself sitting in the middle of a bunch of garage-sale junk, not making any money, that I hatched the plan to sell my great-grandmother's spooky watch. I mean, it was just sitting around in the back of my wardrobe, doing nothing useful ...

'Tell you what, Tony!' said Dad and wiped a crumb from his cheek. 'Why don't we go shopping now? As a reward for all your hard work.'

'Really?' I was so surprised I almost couldn't speak.

'Just let me have a shower,' said Dad, and disappeared.

I could hardly believe it. *Just a quick trip to the shops*, I thought, *and my life will be perfect.*

How wrong I was.

SALE!!! THIS WEEK ONLY!

Posters and streamers were everywhere at the games shop. It looked like a party. But it wasn't until I saw a big red star slapped on the game I was planning to buy, that I really got into the mood. 15% OFF!

'I think I can afford an extra game disc,' I said to Dad.

He looked dazed by all the signs and flashing lights. If he'd been a cartoon character he would have had spinning spiral eyes.

'If you say so, Tony,' Dad muttered.

I grabbed everything I needed before he could change his mind.

The guy at the counter picked up my game and frowned. He glanced over his shoulder then looked at me. 'You know, I shouldn't be telling you this, but that game's on special because it's almost out of date,' he said. 'They're bringing out a new version next week.'

A new version? Now that the guy mentioned it, I remembered Nico saying something about new gear coming out. Imagine what he'd say if I was the first to get it! But at the same time, I'd waited so long for this. I was so, so close . . .

I looked at Dad.

He shrugged. 'It's your money, sonny-boy. Your decision,' he said.

It's my money. The wad of notes felt heavy in my hand. For a moment I thought about what I'd done to get them.

'Okay, I'll take it!' I said quickly, so that I wouldn't have to think it through anymore.

The next thing I knew, I was handing over the cash and picking up a big box with two games discs balanced on top. It almost felt *too* easy, as if I'd just swapped some paper for the solution to all the problems of the universe.

All the way home in the car I read the instruction manual. I couldn't believe the console was really mine. My very own, that I'd be able to play whenever I wanted. Maybe I'd even get good enough to beat the guys!

'Do you want any help setting it up?' Dad asked when we got home. He looked relieved when I told him I'd be fine.

My cat Suki appeared as I was sorting out the colour-coded cords. She touched her nose to the console before rubbing against my arm.

Soon it was ready. Brilliant! I picked a disc, humming to myself while I inserted it into the console. I could hardly believe this was happening. The controller felt amazing in my hands.

'Isn't it beautiful, Suki,' I whispered. 'And it's all mine. This is my console. This is my game. This is my controller.'

It was when the opening screen flashed up that I first noticed something strange: a weird kind of fizzy feeling in the air, like how it feels when a thunderstorm is looming. The hairs on my arms were standing on end and so was Suki's white fur.

But I was too busy selecting 'single player' to worry about any of that. The console was flashing green, the screen was alive with colour and sound. I was playing! I was playing my very own—

Zap!

In a flash of something – not light, more like a sudden burst of electricity – the game switched off.

I was left staring at a screen showing nothing but snow. What was going on?

Suki looked at me. I looked at Suki. She sniffed the screen then wandered away.

I pushed the power button, but nothing happened.

I jiggled all the cords and pushed them in hard. Nothing.

There was still a fizz in the air around me. The hairs on my arms were standing on end. I looked slowly around the room. What could be doing that?

I pulled the connections apart then set the game up again. But no matter how slowly I went, how carefully I worked, I couldn't get it to turn on.

I was still pushing buttons when Suki wandered up for another pat. She turned into a total fuzz ball as she stepped over the game console. It would have been funny except right then I felt like crying.

My new game was totally kaput. Blank. Dead.

'Must be a faulty cord,' said Dad and jiggled it in the power socket, squinting and nodding.

'That must be it,' I said, glad that the static electricity had disappeared.

Dad looked at his watch, then at his glass of cider bubbling quietly where he'd set it down on top of the TV. 'Well, looks like we're heading back to the shops, eh?'

My dad's not all that bad really.

It was late in the day by the time we got home with the new cord.

Suki was asleep on the carpet near the TV. I lifted the console out of the box, and felt it straight away – that strange buzz in the air. Suki looked as though she'd stuck her paw in a power point, but she didn't wake up.

All the hairs on my arms were standing up again. Freaky. It felt like a super-charge of static electricity. But I hadn't plugged anything in yet, so where could it be coming from?

The sound of the front door slamming was followed by Mum's voice. 'Pizza's here!'

Yum. I made straight for the door out of the rumpus room. As soon as I was a few steps from the console the hairs on my arms went down. So did Suki's fur. That couldn't be a coincidence. Could it? It seemed too *deliberate*.

Just to see what would happen, I stepped closer to the console again. Suki's fur stood on end again.

If I hadn't known better I would have started thinking something, or someone, didn't want me to set up this game . . .

I stepped away from the game console. Suki's fur went back to normal.

I stepped closer again. Suki turned into a fuzz ball.

Double weird. It was almost like a game of hot and cold: *warm, warmer . . . now you're boiling hot*. Except this was more like *weird, weirder . . . stop being so weird and spooking me out!*

'Tony, dinner!' came Mum's voice, louder this time.

I was sort of glad to race out of the room.

In the kitchen, Mum was handing out pieces of pizza on plates. I always have margarita. I sat down and bit straight into the best part of the slice – the point of the triangle. Poppy was talking about her callisthenics exams.

'Can you stop talking with your mouth full?' Clio said. 'It's making me sick.'

Poppy swallowed. 'Shut up, Clio. I'm allowed to be happy, alright?'

'I didn't say you weren't,' mumbled Poppy.

'Girls, please!' said Mum.

Dad raised his eyebrows at Mum, and she rolled her eyes. There's always something going on between Clio and Poppy.

'How's the game going?' Dad said to me.

'Ah . . . getting there,' I said slowly.

'Good,' said Dad and nodded. Poppy and Clio were both frowning at their plates and not looking at anyone.

I helped myself to a second piece. Something weird sure was going on with the game. It almost seemed as if it was happening for a reason. As if someone was doing it on purpose . . .

Someone who knew what I'd done to get the money . . .

I put my pizza down, feeling a bit queasy. 'So ah . . . Dad, what was she like? Our great-grandmother, I mean,' I asked.

'What was she like?' said Dad and wiped his mouth with a napkin. 'I don't know. The last time I saw her I was a teenager.'

He took another bite as if he expected that to be enough of an answer. But Mum kept looking at him, and I did too. I really wanted to know. Even Poppy and Clio had stopped frowning at their plates and were waiting for Dad to keep going.

He looked at the pizza in his hand. 'Well, she

used to cook amazing food, but . . .' He shook his head and his voice drifted off.

'But what?' I prodded.

'Well, she was a bit . . . bossy, really,' he said. 'She was used to getting her own way. I was a bit scared of making her angry, you know?'

I swallowed and glanced down, feeling queasy. 'Yeah . . . I think I know what you mean.'

If she was here right now, she'd have a *pretty good* reason to be angry.

Could this be happening because of what I'd done with my great-grandmother's watch?

Surely not! It was all just a coincidence, right? The console stopped working because something was wrong with it, not because of where the money came from . . .

After dinner I went back to the rumpus room, feeling silly. I didn't want to be disrespectful or anything, but my great-grandmother was dead and buried on the other side of the world. Maybe she had been a bit bossy while she was alive. But there was no way she could know what I had done with her watch. I didn't need to worry. Right?

I gathered my courage, picked up the cord and plugged it in. Maybe our next-door neighbour had put up a new aerial or something. Maybe some kind of interference was the reason the hairs on my arms were standing on end.

Even my teeth had started to tingle. But I ignored it, plugged everything in and turned the console on.

When the first screen appeared, I hit SINGLE PLAYER. Then START GAME.

Zap!

Everything died. Again.

Everything, that was, except my heart – it was racing like never before. If someone was trying to freak me out, they were doing a pretty good job!

It was hard to put my finger on what it was, but I could feel *something* in the room. With me.

She was here. And something told me that my great-grandmother wasn't the kind of person who liked electronic games. Especially not ones that had been bought using money earned from selling her stuff.

I cleared my throat. 'Ah ... hello?' I whispered.

No floating great-grandmothers appeared.

Just to be sure, I added, '*Yasou*?' which was about as much Greek as I could manage right then. There was no response, but the air felt clear and the hairs on my arms were flat.

If my great-grandmother *was* somehow here, if she could see what was going on, then I was pretty sure she didn't like what she was seeing – her youngest great-grandson in the land of plenty in Australia, living it up on her precious jewellery . . .

Not that I felt as if I was exactly *living it up*. In fact, I was feeling a bit sick, as if that fuzzy electricity had zapped my gut. Bleugh.

And I had a feeling it wouldn't go away until I fixed what I'd done.

I had to buy back the evil-eye watch, and that meant returning the game.

6

'Where's Dad?' I asked Mum the next morning in the kitchen.

She yawned, leaning against the bench. 'Your dad's sick. Says he's coming down with something. He's going to try and sleep it off.'

'Sick?' I said. 'Like . . . queasy?'

Mum frowned. 'Do you have it too, Tony?'

'No, no,' I lied. *Was my great-grandmother angry at Dad too?*

The jug clicked and Mum poured water into her mug.

'Can I get a lift into the shops?' I asked. 'There's some stuff I need to do.'

The spoon clanked against the mug as Mum stirred. 'Didn't you spend all your money yesterday?'

'Yeah . . . it's just . . . I changed my mind.'

Mum stopped stirring and went to say

something. Then she sighed. 'Alright, I'm going to the supermarket later. Come with me then.'

Great. Operation keep-the-ghost-happy was on track.

The games shop was crowded. A new sign had been added to all the others:

$390.90!!! ONE WEEK TO GO! THE LASTEST GAMING TECHNOLOGY! ONLY $390.90!!!

Whatever. I just wanted to hand over the game and get my money back. I was glad to see a different shop assistant. She didn't stop chewing gum the whole time I was in there. At least she took the console and games back and didn't ask any questions. Once I had the wad of money in my pocket, I started feeling better. Everything would be okay.

The jewellery shop was a bit of a walk up the hill and around the corner. I was panting by the time I reached the door.

Just like the day before, I went in and blinked in the dim lights, waiting for my eyes to adjust.

Then I saw it. The watch was sitting in a

display case – a single, unblinking eye staring at me. The blue face glowed like a shimmering ocean. It had a shiny new gold plaited band. The price tag said $550.

'Back so soon?' asked the shop owner.

I hadn't even seen him until he spoke.

'I changed my mind. I need it back.'

'Is that so?' the old man said slowly. His keys rattled against the glass as he unlocked the display case. 'I'm quite pleased with how it came up,' he said, and placed the watch carefully on the counter.

'Yeah, that's great.' I pushed the wad of money towards him. 'Thanks.'

The old man licked his lips and started counting.

I tried to ignore the blue eye staring up at me.

'There's not enough here, I'm afraid,' he said. 'You need five hundred and fifty if you want to buy that watch.'

My jaw dropped. 'What? But I sold it to you for *three* hundred and fifty just yesterday!'

'Sorry, young man,' said the owner. 'That's

commerce for you. It's called "value adding". I bought it from you, added value, and now I'm going to sell it for a profit.' He squished his lips together, trying to hide a smile.

'But . . . but . . .' I looked at the eye, sitting there. Watching. 'But I *need* it back!'

'Then you *need* to find another two hundred dollars,' he said. This time he did smile. 'Maybe you could ask your parents.'

I sure didn't like this guy. 'Just give me some time. Okay?'

'I can call you if someone else shows interest in the watch. How about that?'

'Thanks,' I said as I wrote down my number. *Thanks for nothing.*

As I walked down the hill to the supermarket, I felt a familiar queasiness in my gut. My heart was beating fast too, but not just from walking this time. This was a disaster!

I needed money. Lots of it. But I had no idea how to get it. I didn't have anything worth selling, and I couldn't tell my parents what I had done. How was I going to get the extra money to buy back the watch?

The only thing I knew for sure was that my great-grandmother wasn't happy.

Please don't be angry! I begged. *Don't make my family sick! I'll get your watch back. I promise. I'll get it back . . .*

But how?

7

Back at home I sneaked a quick peek into Dad's room. He was sitting up in bed, sipping lemonade and reading the newspaper. He didn't seem too sick.

But that didn't solve my big problem. How was I going to earn the extra money to buy back the watch? I had the three hundred and fifty dollars from returning the game, and twelve dollars seventy-five from the garage sale.

That made $362.75. I counted it all out just to be sure.

It was all there. But I was still $187.25 short.

How could I make that kind of money *without* asking my parents?

I started thinking about selling my stuff online – even stuff that I still wanted. My cricket bat? My clock radio? My complete set of Monster Mayhem books? But what would I say to Mum and Dad when they realised all my things were missing?

Around lunchtime I wandered into the kitchen with an eye for valuable items. We had an old breadmaker in a cupboard somewhere that no one used anymore.

But I didn't get around to opening any cupboards. Lying open on the bench was a worn-out recipe book. I recognised it straight away. It was the one Dad had inherited from my great-grandmother.

A shiver ran up my spine. Was she trying to give me another sign?

I didn't even want to go near the thing, but at the same time it was hard not to take a look. The pages were all tattered and splashed with stains. It smelled ripe and sort of spicy. I looked closer . . .

'Tony?'

I jumped, half-expecting it to be my great-grandmother. Thank goodness. It was just Mum.

'Amazing, isn't it,' she said, and delicately turned a page. 'There's a whole lifetime of recipes in here.'

The next page was covered with a magazine cut-out, folded neatly to fit. It was in Greek, of course. One of the recipes had been crossed out and another had been double-ticked.

'I'm thinking of making something from here for Easter lunch next week,' said Mum. 'What do you think? Your dad can help with the translation.'

I nodded, watching the book as Mum kept turning pages. 'Yeah, good,' I mumbled.

The paper crackled slightly as it was moved. 'There's meant to be a recipe in here that your great-grandmother invented,' said Mum quietly. 'I wonder which one it is.'

The next page had an old recipe card stuck on it, but half of the ingredients had been crossed out and others added.

Mum looked at me. 'Don't let on to your dad that I told you this,' she said, 'but this recipe book was meant to be for you, Tony. Your dad was worried that you'd be upset and swapped his watch for the recipe book.'

Right. No wonder Dad was feeling sick. My ghost great-grandmother was peeved with him too.

'Maybe she thought you'd become a great cook just like her!' said Mum. She squeezed my shoulders, then opened a cupboard and started pulling out pots.

I looked at the recipe book again. I was meant to inherit this?

The next page didn't have anything stuck down. It was a recipe written out entirely in pencil. It was faded but still easy to see. My great-grandmother's handwriting.

I couldn't take my eyes off that page. Years ago, on the other side of the world, my great-grandmother had guided a pencil to form each of these letters. Had she been wearing the watch when she wrote them?

A strange feeling came over me then – not

fizziness or anything spooky. It was more a kind of sadness. It made me think. Not so long ago, my great-grandmother was cooking, eating, living . . .

In some ways, I didn't blame her for being angry about the watch. It made her seem, well, gutsy, to be standing up for herself.

'See if you can find any cookie recipes,' came Mum's muffled voice from inside the cupboard. 'Your dad says she used to sell them to the whole village.'

I flipped a page, then stopped. *She used to sell them to the whole village . . .*

Could I do that? Could I make cookies and then sell them?

I wasn't a very good cook, but I knew how to follow a recipe. Would anyone want to buy something that I had cooked?

My mind ticked through the possibilities. Maybe I could do an order form and hand it out at school.

Mum had a pot on the stove and was looking at me funny. 'Everything okay?' she asked.

'Yeah,' I nodded, slow at first then faster and faster. Everything wasn't okay *yet*, but maybe it would be soon.

Three days later, I had a pile of order forms and bags of ingredients on the kitchen bench. Operation keep-the-ghost-happy was back on track. There were even more orders than I'd dared hope, enough to make the money I needed and a bit more. But I still had to bake the cookies, and I was nervous about that. I was going to have to make double batches, or even triple, to get all the orders cooked in time.

Dad was feeling better and had helped me translate a biscuit recipe from the old cookbook. He was having trouble with one of the ingredients until Mum walked past, took one look at the English translation and said, 'It must be baking powder.' I was impressed.

At the back of my mind the whole time I imagined my great-grandmother hanging around – well, hovering, or whatever it was that she did – watching what was going on. She didn't send any more electricity to make everything go weird, though. A good sign, I decided.

That was, until the afternoon when I started to cook.

I felt it as soon as I pulled a mixing bowl out of the cupboard – the fizz of electricity in the air. It hit me with a rush of surprise and confusion. What? Didn't she want me cooking?

I stopped myself from gesturing rudely at thin air. Instead, I humphed loud enough for anyone who might be listening to hear it, and put the bowl back.

Right on cue, the fizziness faded.

I wasn't expecting this. For a while I frowned at the packets of ingredients spread out in front of me. They looked so . . . *ready* to be made into something more than just flour and sugar. I'd even used my own money to buy them.

I put my hands on my hips. My great-grandmother might be bossy. She might be stubborn. But her youngest great-grandson could be stubborn too.

Gritting my teeth I pulled the bowl out of the cupboard again.

Zap went the air around me. My hair stood on end. Even my jumper felt prickly. I ignored it and picked up a bar of butter. My teeth began to tingle and I started feeling dizzy. My great-grandmother was hitting me with the works.

What was her problem? I put the butter down and bit my lip.

It wasn't as if she had gone all fizzy on me when I'd printed out the order forms. Or when I'd bought the ingredients. Maybe it wasn't exactly the *cooking* that she didn't like. Maybe it was something as simple as . . . the mixing bowl.

I put the bowl back in the cupboard for the second time, and took a deep breath. With slow, deliberate steps, I moved around the kitchen.

Then, near a corner cupboard, I sensed something. It wasn't a zap this time, more a kind of pulsing around me. It felt warm. An invitation.

As soon as I opened the cupboard, I knew what my great-grandmother was after. It was the electric mixer. Maybe she wasn't opposed to technology all the time. I pulled it out and the air stayed normal.

I went to plug the power cord in . . .

Zap went the air.

Okay. I put the cord down. So she wanted me to set it all up *before* I plugged it in.

'Do you want any help?' Mum was hovering, peering at the electric mixer.

'Ah . . . not yet,' I said. 'I'll let you know.'

I had the feeling that I was going to be getting all the help I needed.

At first as I began to mix the ingredients, I kept getting zapped – like little slaps on the wrist – when I did something wrong. *Too much! Too hot! Enough!* But soon I began to get a feel for what my great-grandmother liked in the kitchen – she preferred wooden spoons to plastic ones and liked a low flame on the stove. She especially liked it when I cleaned up as I went along.

It was the best feeling when I shaped my first cookie. I'd rolled out a piece of dough into a fat worm shape, then folded it in half and twisted.

When I placed it on the baking tray, the air pulsed warmly. First try and she was happy!

The cookies all came out perfect, every batch. Even Clio and Poppy hung around being friendly so they could have a taste.

I worked really hard that day and I had to get up early to cook the next morning. But when it was all finished, I had to admit that cooking with my great-grandmother had been great fun.

On Easter Sunday I helped Mum cook lunch. Not because I had to, because I wanted to. I had already used the money I'd earned to buy back the watch. I couldn't stop grinning at that nasty old shop owner as he counted out the money.

Then I brought the watch home and gave it to Dad. 'Here,' I said. 'I thought you might like it now.'

Dad was so surprised that he didn't know what to say. He nodded at the watch, then looked up at me with a strange look on his face.

Now it was propped up in a clear plastic case, sitting on the photo shelf in the lounge room. I imagined it looking out at everything that went on.

The watch was back, safe and sound, but I couldn't help checking for signs that my great-grandmother was still around. Now that I ... well, sort of *knew* her a bit, I didn't want her to go.

But the last time I'd felt her was when I'd put the cookies into bags. She'd sent me on a long hunt to find a red ribbon in the bottom of a drawer. The bags had looked really good tied up with ribbons. But that had been three days before.

As I cooked with Mum I kept bracing myself for a zap on the wrist or a warm pulse. At one point I even chose a plastic spoon to see if anything happened. Nothing did. After a while I swapped the plastic spoon for a wooden one.

I hoped that my great-grandmother was still around, but that wasn't the only reason why I wanted to help cook. Now that I had a feel for it, I didn't want to stop. There was something about the process – the transformation of ingredients – that I found fascinating. The way floppy, sticky cookie dough went firm and crunchy just after being hot for a while. Who was the first person who came up with that idea? How did they work out what would happen? Who first decided to mix flour and egg, and how did they realise that something like yeast would make dough grow bigger and softer with heat? Before people knew how different ingredients worked, it must have been strange trying to cook. The first time someone baked bread in the coals of a fire, it must have seemed like magic.

I couldn't stop looking through the old Greek recipe book either. It seemed to hold the ideas and experiments of so many people. Starting with the ones who first worked out how to cook with fire, or how to make dough, then adding all the other people who'd come after them who'd tried adding sugar, or sultanas or whatever, to make it taste even better. And then my great-grand-mother had come along and collected recipes, changing them or adding something new and finally passing it all on to me and Mum.

It made me feel, I don't know, *lucky* to have that book. It seemed like something worth looking after.

After lunch we sat around the table, too full to keep eating but too relaxed to leave. Even Clio and Poppy were in a good mood.

I leaned over and snuck a piece of lettuce from the salad bowl. The tang of the dressing tasted good but it needed a bit more salt. Maybe next time I could add some soy sauce . . .

Dad shifted in his chair and cleared his throat. 'I have a confession to make, everyone,' he said. 'Your great-grandmother didn't just leave you jewellery in her will. She also left a bit of money as a wedding present for each of you when you get married . . .'

'How much?' asked Clio straight away.

Poppy was grinning. 'What does *a bit* mean?'

They looked pretty interested. I was too, though not as much as I would have been two weeks before. I don't plan to ever get married. And now that I had a way to earn my own money, I wasn't so fussed about having it given to me.

'I'm getting to that,' said Dad to the girls. Then he looked at me. Mum was smiling strangely at me too.

'We're very proud of the way you worked this past week, Tony,' said Dad. 'The way you treated your great-grandmother's watch, paying for it to be fixed up.' He looked at Mum, who nodded. 'We think you've been very mature with your money . . . mature enough to manage a bit of your own. And since it'll be such a long time until you get married . . .'

'And there's no guarantee that you will . . .' interrupted Mum.

'We thought the inheritance money would mean more to you now,' finished Dad.

Really? Everyone was looking at me. I wasn't sure if I was imagining it, but something seemed to change in the air. It wasn't fizzy, or even pulsing, but I could still feel *something* . . .

'Come on, Dad!' cried Poppy. 'How much are we talking here?'

'Eight hundred euros shared between the three of you,' said Dad.

That sounded like a whole heap of money, but no one knew how many dollars were in one euro. We all started talking at the same time.

'Calm down, you lot!' called Dad. He pulled out his mobile and started pressing buttons. 'If I find out the exchange rate ... euros into Australian dollars. ... then I subtract a commission for exchanging the money ... and divide that amount by three ...'

Dad looked at the screen and raised his eyebrows. 'Well son, nothing to sneeze at, eh?'

As I leaned forward, the sense of *something* increased in the air around me. It was good to have it back. It made me feel safe somehow ... part of something.

'How much, Tony?' asked Poppy.

I looked at the screen and burst out laughing. It read 390.90 – the exact price of the new-release game console. I had a feeling that this one would work fine.

Mum leaned forward. 'We want you to buy

something that will remind you of your great-grandmother.'

'No problem!' I grinned. It was pretty much guaranteed that I'd think of my great-grand-mother each time I played my new game . . .

Each time I turned it on, and it didn't go *zap!*

ABOUT THE AUTHOR

Thalia grew up on a farm on the outskirts of Melbourne. After a stint as a dancer she edited websites and travel guides. But her biggest passion has always been writing. Thalia has published multiple books in the Go Girl! series, as well as the non-fiction children's book *It's True! Sleep Makes You Smarter!* (which *is* true, in case you're wondering). She has also published two novels in the Girlfriend Fiction series, *Step Up and Dance* and *What Supergirl Did Next*.

These days she lives in north-eastern Victoria with her husband and two children, as well as two cats, three frogs and a big family of micro bats. She is currently trying to think up a logical reason why time travellers from the future haven't popped in yet to say hi.